U0085006

序　言

在大學入學考試英文這一科，想得高分，除了要多背單字之外，成語也是不可忽視的一環。熟背成語，不僅在慣用語部分能拿滿分，而且對於提升「克漏字測驗」、「文意選填」、「篇章結構」的答題能力，及「閱讀測驗」的理解力方面，都有莫大的助益。

爲了幫助同學，能在短期內精通大學入試必考成語，我們特別收集歷屆大學聯考、學科能力測驗、指定科目考試，以及各大規模模擬考試中的英文試題，經由電腦統計，選出在考試中，最常出現的 1000 個關鍵成語，彙編成這本「升大學成語 1000」。本書的每一個成語都非常重要。

書中的成語依其用法，分為副詞、動詞、形容詞，及其他用法的成語四大類，同時，每個成語均附有例句，清楚說明該成語的用法，每四頁即附有 **Check List**，可供同學自我評量，驗收學習成果。此外，**熟讀每單元後的「同義成語」歸納，能幫助您舉一反三，觸類旁通**，寫英文作文時，文思泉湧，讓文章更生動、更有變化。

　　這本書是由謝靜芳老師擔任總指揮，外籍老師 Laura E. Stewart 及林銀姿老師負責校對，白雪嬌小姐設計封面，黃淑貞小姐負責排版，王淑平小姐協助打字，王婷玉小姐及洪淑娟小姐協助整理資料，我們感謝這些工作人員的辛勞。本書雖經審慎校對，力求正確無誤，但仍恐有疏漏之處，誠盼各界先進不吝批評指正。

劉　毅

PART 1 ▶ 副詞用法的成語

⋯⋯ ★ STEP 1 ★ ⋯⋯

☐ **above all** 最重要的是

Be careful on your trip. *Above all*, don't drink and drive.

☐ **after all** 畢竟

It's easy for parents to over-schedule their children's lives; *after all*, parents don't want their children to grow up dumb.

☐ **ahead of schedule** 進度超前

To the surprise of everyone, the project was completed *ahead of schedule*.

☐ **ahead of time** 事先

If you intend to make a tour of any of the big factories, you had better make an appointment *ahead of time*.

☐ **all at once** 突然地

All at once there was a tremendous crash.

☐ **all but** 幾乎 (= *almost*)

The street was *all but* deserted.

☐ **all of a sudden** 突然地

During the first few seconds of the earthquake, many buildings collapsed *all of a sudden*.

☐ **anything but** 絕不;一點也不

The speech was *anything but* interesting. It wasn't long before the audience felt bored.

☐ **around the clock** 二十四小時地

Firefighters are on call virtually *around the clock*. They never seem to be off duty.

☐ **as a matter of fact** 事實上

Judging from his outfit, you might think that he is poor. *As a matter of fact*, he is almost as rich as Bill Gates.

☐ **as follows** 如下

My address is *as follows*.

☐ **as good as** 就像⋯一樣

(= *almost the same as*)

A little paint will make your car look *as good as* new.

☐ **as it happens** 不湊巧地

As it happened, my grandma was not at home that day.

☐ **as luck would have it** 碰巧

As luck would have it, I arrived in Chicago just when my sister got there.

☑ **as the crow flies** 成一直線地

(= *in a straight line*)

It is ten miles from Hartford to Manchester, *as the crow flies*.

☑ **as the world goes** 按一般標準來說

He is a good man *as the world goes*.

☑ **as well** 也 (= *too*)

Adolescence might be agonizingly stormy and stressful, but it could be a kind of rebirth *as well*.

☑ **as yet** 到目前為止；至今

As yet, little has been discovered about the causes of this disease.

☑ **at all** 究竟；到底

It isn't so much whether he works hard; the question is whether he works *at all*.

🏛 Check List

☐ as yet _____

☐ ahead of time _____

☐ as a matter of fact _____

☐ all but _____

☐ all at once _____

☐ around the clock _____

☐ as well _____

☐ as the world goes _____

☐ as it happens _____

☐ anything but _____

☐ after all _____

☐ above all _____

☐ all of a sudden _____

☐ as follows _____

☐ as the crow flies _____

同義成語

1. *above all*
   = most important of all
   最重要的是

2. *all at once*
   = all of a sudden
   = out of the blue
   = out of a clear blue sky
   = unexpectedly
   = suddenly
   突然地

3. *anything but*
   = on no account
   = by no means
   = far from
   = not in the least
   = not at all
   絕不；一點也不

4. *ahead of time*
   = in advance
   = beforehand
   事先

5. *as a matter of fact*
   = in fact
   = in truth
   = in reality
   = in effect
   = actually
   事實上

6. *as yet*
   = so far
   = until now
   = up to now
   = up to the present time
   到目前為止；至今

⋯⋯ ⭐ STEP 2 ⭐ ⋯⋯

☐ **at all costs** 不惜任何代價

I must get the book *at all costs*.

☐ **at any rate** 無論如何 (= *anyway*)

Our attempt failed, but *at any rate* we learned a lot from the experience.

☐ **at best** 最多；充其量只不過是

These batteries are not good. *At best* they will last only for two months.

☐ **at intervals** 有時

The discussion was so long and exhausting that *at intervals* the speakers stopped for refreshments.

☐ **at last** 最後；終於

After a long debate, we reached a conclusion *at last*.

☐ **at least** 至少

This coat will cost *at least* two hundred dollars.

☐ **at length** 詳細地；終於

The scientist spoke *at length* to the audience about the dangers of global warming.

☐ **at** *one's* **convenience**
在某人方便的時候

You may pay me *at your convenience*.

☐ **at random** 隨便地；任意地

The professor picked some students *at random* from the class and asked them to help with the experiment.

☐ **at second hand** 間接地

This information may be unreliable since I got it *at second hand*.

☐ **at short notice** 在短時間內；立刻

Our landlord announced that we should
move out of our apartment *at short notice*.

☐ **at times** 有時候；偶爾 (= *sometimes*)

A person who forgets *at times*, forgets
occasionally.

☐ **at will** 任意地 (= *at liberty*)

You cannot control the workings of your
heart *at will*.

☐ **back and forth** 來回地

The pendulum of the old clock swung
back and forth.

☐ **be just as well** 不妨

I didn't know he was such a hot-tempered
person. It's *just as well* that I didn't tell
him the truth.

☐ **beyond reach** 在拿不到的地方

Put the cookies up *beyond reach*, so the children won't eat them.

☐ **by a hair's breadth** 差一點

The speeding car missed the child who ran out into the road *by a hair's breadth*.

☐ **by all means** 務必；當然

By all means take a week's vacation.

☐ **by and by** 不久

You will forget him *by and by*.

☐ **by and large** 大體而言

This TV program, *by and large*, introduces viewers to different species of animals.

Check List

- [ ] at any rate　＿＿＿＿＿＿＿
- [ ] at last　＿＿＿＿＿＿＿
- [ ] at second hand　＿＿＿＿＿＿＿
- [ ] be just as well　＿＿＿＿＿＿＿
- [ ] by and large　＿＿＿＿＿＿＿

- [ ] at least　＿＿＿＿＿＿＿
- [ ] at intervals　＿＿＿＿＿＿＿
- [ ] at best　＿＿＿＿＿＿＿
- [ ] at length　＿＿＿＿＿＿＿
- [ ] at short notice　＿＿＿＿＿＿＿

- [ ] by a hair's breadth　＿＿＿＿＿＿＿
- [ ] at times　＿＿＿＿＿＿＿
- [ ] at random　＿＿＿＿＿＿＿
- [ ] beyond reach　＿＿＿＿＿＿＿
- [ ] at will　＿＿＿＿＿＿＿

📖 同義成語

1. *at any rate*
   = in any case
   = come what may
   = on any account
   = anyway
   無論如何

2. *at intervals* 有時
   = at times
   = (every) now and then
   = (every) now and again
   = once in a while
   = occasionally
   = sometimes

3. *at length* 詳細地
   = in full
   = with all the details

4. *at last* 最後;終於
   = at length
   = in the end
   = in the long run
   = eventually
   = finally

5. *back and forth*
   = to and fro
   來回地

6. *by and by* 不久
   = before long
   = after a while
   = shortly
   = soon

7. *by and large*
   = on the whole
   = all in all
   = in general
   = generally
   大體而言

⋯⋯ ⋆ STEP ③ ⋆ ⋯⋯

☐ **by contrast** 對比之下

He had almost failed the exam, but his brother, *by contrast*, had done very well.

☐ **by degrees** 漸漸地

It began to get light, and things were becoming visible *by degrees*.

☐ **by far** 顯然

This is *by far* the most significant discovery we have ever made.

☐ **by halves** 不徹底（= *incompletely*）

Don't do things *by halves*. Persevere!

☐ **by hook or by crook** 不擇手段

(= *by hook or crook*)

Come what may, I must have that house.
So I intend to get it *by hook or by crook*.

☐ **by leaps and bounds** 迅速地

The school's enrollment rate is going up *by leaps and bounds* due to the improvement of the facilities.

☐ **by no means** 絕不

The wine in this country is *by no means* as good as that in France.

☐ **by now** 此時；此刻（已經）

He will be in London *by now*.

□ **by** *oneself* 獨自;靠自己 (= *alone*)

It's very dangerous that he went mountain climbing all *by himself*.

□ **by the way** 順便一提 (= *incidentally*)

We shall expect you at eight o'clock; *by the way*, it's an informal dinner.

□ **by trade** 職業是… (= *by profession*)

The father of Abraham Lincoln was a carpenter *by trade*.

□ **by turns** 輪流地

Jack and I agreed to work at the office on Saturdays *by turns*.

□ **contrary to** 與~相反

Contrary to the popular belief that classical music is too complex, it achieves a simplicity that only a genius can create.

☐ **every now and then** 偶爾;有時
(= *now and then*)

Every now and then they go to a movie together.

☐ **far and away** 無疑地;非常地

Roy is *far and away* the most competent person in our company.

☐ **far and wide** 到處 (= *everywhere*)

They searched *far and wide* for the missing mountain climbers.

☐ **far from** 一點也不;絕不 (= *not at all*)

Her room was *far from* being tidy at that time. It was in a terrible mess.

☐ **for ages** 很久 (= *for a long time*)

Where have you been? I haven't seen you *for ages*.

Check List

- [ ] for ages _____
- [ ] every now and then _____
- [ ] by the way _____
- [ ] by halves _____
- [ ] by degrees _____

- [ ] by leaps and bounds _____
- [ ] by turns _____
- [ ] far and wide _____
- [ ] far from _____
- [ ] contrary to _____

- [ ] by *oneself* _____
- [ ] by far _____
- [ ] by hook or by crook _____
- [ ] by trade _____
- [ ] far and away _____

📖 同義成語

1. *be degrees*
   = gradually
   = bit by bit
   = little by little
   = inch by inch
   漸漸地

2. *by hook or by crook*
   = by any means
   不擇手段

3. *by leaps and bounds*
   = very rapidly
   迅速地

4. *for ages* 很久
   = for a long time

5. *every now and then*
   = every now and again
   = at times
   = at intervals
   = once in a while
   = occasionally
   = sometimes

   偶爾；有時

⋯⋅ ★ **STEP 4** ★ ⋅⋯

☐ **for better or for worse**

不論是好是壞；不論甘苦

After going steady for years, he promised
to marry her *for better or for worse*.

☐ **for good**　永遠（= *forever*）

He hoped that the repairs would stop the
leak *for good*.

☐ **for nothing**　免費地（= *for free*）

You don't have to pay.　You can have this
book *for nothing*.

☐ **for** *one's* **life**　拼命地

He ran *for his life* when the bear
approached.

☐ **for my part** 就我而言

(= *as far as I am concerned*)

For my part, I don't mind where we eat.

☐ **for the first time** 生平第一次

Everything was exciting to me when I visited Spain *for the first time*.

☐ **from now on** 從今以後

The teacher told her student, "Please don't cheat *from now on*."

☐ **from scratch** 從一無所有

(= *from nothing*)

Bill Gates built Microsoft, the foremost software company in the world, *from scratch*.

☐ **hand in hand** 手牽手；形影相隨

Selfishness and unhappiness often go *hand in hand*.

☐ **in a flash** 立刻

We were watching the bird eat the crumbs; then I sneezed, and it was gone *in a flash*.

☐ **in a jiffy** 立刻

Please wait ten more minutes. I'll be back *in a jiffy*.

☐ **in all** 總計

There are 1100 boys and girls *in all* in our school.

☐ **in a row** 連續地

He came into the pub and had three drinks *in a row*.

☐ **in addition** 此外

The taxi driver drove recklessly and was unfriendly to me; *in addition*, the cab was very dirty.

☐ **in advance**　事先

If you want to see a dentist, you must make an appointment *in advance*.

☐ **in detail**　詳細地

We'll have to examine the data from our last experiment *in detail* before we know what went wrong.

☐ **in due course**　到適當的時候

Sow the seeds now and *in due course* you will have the flowers.

☐ **in fact**　事實上

He doesn't mind. *In fact*, he's very pleased.

☐ **in general**　一般說來

Women *in general* like to shop for new clothes.

🏛 Check List

- ☐ in due course　　　＿＿＿＿＿＿
- ☐ in a jiffy　　　　　＿＿＿＿＿＿
- ☐ for the first time　　＿＿＿＿＿＿
- ☐ for good　　　　　　＿＿＿＿＿＿
- ☐ for *one's* part　　　　＿＿＿＿＿＿

- ☐ in a flash　　　　　＿＿＿＿＿＿
- ☐ in detail　　　　　　＿＿＿＿＿＿
- ☐ in fact　　　　　　＿＿＿＿＿＿
- ☐ in addition　　　　　＿＿＿＿＿＿
- ☐ from scratch　　　　＿＿＿＿＿＿

- ☐ for *one's* life　　　　＿＿＿＿＿＿
- ☐ for nothing　　　　　＿＿＿＿＿＿
- ☐ from now on　　　　＿＿＿＿＿＿
- ☐ in a row　　　　　　＿＿＿＿＿＿
- ☐ hand in hand　　　　＿＿＿＿＿＿

同義成語

1. **for better or for worse**
   = through thick and thin
   = through good times and bad times
   不論甘苦；不論是好是壞

2. **for good** 永遠
   = forever
   = permanently

3. **in a row** 連續地
   = in succession
   = successively

4. **in all** 總計
   = in total
   = all told

5. **in a flash** 立刻
   = in a jiffy
   = in an instant
   = in a minute
   = in no time
   = right away
   = at once
   = without delay
   = immediately

6. **in addition** 此外
   = besides
   = moreover
   = furthermore
   = what's more

7. **for nothing** 免費
   = for free
   = free of charge
   = without charge
   = without payment

⟨ ★ **STEP 5** ★ ⟩

☐ **in no time** 立刻

We'll do fine. We'll be bosom buddies *in no time*.

☐ **in no way** 絕不

Without the friction between their feet and the ground, people would *in no way* be able to walk.

☐ **in other words** 換句話說

We should use computers wisely. *In other words*, we should not use them to invade someone's privacy.

☐ **in particular** 尤其是

Pollution is getting worse in many countries, industrialized countries *in particular*.

☐ **in person**　親自（= *personally*）

Come *in person*; do not write or phone.

☐ **in perspective**　以正確的眼光

No matter how tough the problem is, we have to keep it *in perspective*.

☐ **in return**　作為回報

A foreign student sometimes does small jobs around the house *in return* for his room and meals.

☐ **in some measure**　有點；有幾分

His failure is *in some measure* due to lack of confidence.

☐ **in the distance**　在遠方

You can see the ancient ruins *in the distance*.

☐ **in the long run** 到最後；終於

I am sure that *in the long run* he will prove to be your best friend.

☐ **in the nick of time** 正是時候

(= *just in time*)

You got here *in the nick of time*—the train is leaving.

☐ **in time** 及時

Do you think we will be *in time* for the plane?

☐ **in turn** 依序地

Our teacher made every student get up and speak *in turn* in our speech class.

☐ **in vain** 徒勞無功

We tried to make him change his mind but *in vain*.

☐ **little better than** (= *almost as bad as*)
差不多等於；幾乎和～一樣的糟

Mike is always unwilling to return the
money he borrows. He is *little better
than* a thief.

☐ **little by little** 漸漸地

Practice every day, and your English will
improve *little by little*.

☐ **more importantly** 更重要的是

We can always work toward improving
our self-control, and, *more importantly*,
we can help others do the same.

☐ **more or less** 多多少少

I understand what the teacher said *more
or less*. I just have a few questions.

🏛 Check List

☐ in no way _____

☐ in perspective _____

☐ in the nick of time _____

☐ more importantly _____

☐ in other words _____

☐ in vain _____

☐ little better than _____

☐ in some measure _____

☐ in no time _____

☐ in particular _____

☐ in the long run _____

☐ little by little _____

☐ more or less _____

☐ in turn _____

☐ in return _____

同義成語

1. *in no way* 絕不
   = by no means
   = on no account
   = far from
   = not at all

2. *in some measure*
   = to some extent
   = to some degree
   有點；有幾分

3. *little by little*
   = bit by bit
   = inch by inch
   = by degrees
   = gradually
   漸漸地

4. *in the long run*
   = in the end
   = at length
   = at last
   = eventually
   = finally
   到最後；終於

5. *in vain*
   = without effect
   = to no avail
   = to no purpose
   徒勞無功

⟶ **STEP ⑥** ⟵

☐ **needless to say** 不用說

He never pays attention in class. *Needless to say*, he failed in the final exam.

☐ **no doubt** 無疑地

No doubt he will succeed in everything he does since he works so hard.

☐ **no wonder** 難怪

He is an Olympic medallist. *No wonder* his son is so excellent in sports.

☐ **not in the least** 一點也不 (*= not at all*)

The naughty student is the last person Mary wants to see. She does *not* like him *in the least*.

☐ **nothing but** 只是 (= *only*)

Ever since I was a child, my inherent recklessness has brought me *nothing but* trouble.

☐ **nothing less than** 簡直就是

Hugging helps the immune system, reduces stress and has no unpleasant side effects. It is *nothing less than* a miracle drug.

☐ **nothing more than** 只是

He feels a little sad. What he needs is *nothing more than* a little consolation.

☐ **off duty** 不執勤；下班 (↔ *on duty*)

Though the policeman was *off duty* at the time, he recognized the man as a wanted criminal and arrested him.

☐ **on and off** 斷斷續續地

It has been raining *on and off* since morning.

☐ **on earth** 究竟；到底

What *on earth* is the matter? Which one of you can tell me?

☐ **on end** 不停地；連續地 (= *continuously*)

They will explore the seashore for days *on end*.

☐ **on hand** 在手邊；可用

I happened to have your application *on hand* at that moment.

☐ **on no account** 絕不

On no account are you to touch an electrical appliance with wet hands.

☐ **on purpose** 故意地

Sometimes young people turn against their parents *on purpose*.

☐ **on the contrary** 相反地

You didn't bother me. *On the contrary*, I like your company.

☐ **on the other hand** 另一方面

I live outside the city. It's a nice place to live but, *on the other hand*, it takes me a long time to get to work.

☐ **on the spot** 當場

The criminal was caught *on the spot*.

☐ **on the whole** 整體而言

This story, *on the whole*, is fascinating: there are many interesting characters in it.

🏛 Check List

- ☐ nothing but _____
- ☐ on and off _____
- ☐ on no account _____
- ☐ on the spot _____
- ☐ needless to say _____

- ☐ on end _____
- ☐ nothing more than _____
- ☐ no wonder _____
- ☐ no doubt _____
- ☐ nothing less than _____

- ☐ on earth _____
- ☐ on the contrary _____
- ☐ on the other hand _____
- ☐ on hand _____
- ☐ off duty _____

📖 同義成語

1. *Needless to say,* ~
   = It goes without
   saying that ~
   不用說，~

2. *no doubt*
   = beyond doubt
   = without doubt
   = without a doubt
   = undoubtedly
   無疑地

3. *nothing but* 只是
   = no more than
   = only

4. *on and off*
   = off and on
   = intermittently
   斷斷續續

5. *on earth*
   = in the world
   究竟；到底

6. *on hand* 在手邊
   = on tap
   = within reach

7. *on no account*
   = by no means
   絕不

8. *on purpose*
   = deliberately
   = purposely
   = intentionally
   故意地

9. *on the spot* 當場
   = on the scene

⋯ ★ **STEP 7** ★ ⋯

☐ **on time** 準時

I do my best to be *on time* for school every morning.

☐ **on trial** 接受審判；試驗中

She was going *on trial* for fraud and theft.

☐ **once and for all** 只此一次；堅決地

I'm telling you *once and for all* that you must not do such a stupid thing again.

☐ **once in a blue moon** 很少有

It is only *once in a blue moon* that you get an opportunity like that. You should do your very best to fully take advantage of it.

☑ **once in a while** 偶爾 (= *occasionally*)

Previously I saw him very often but now
he comes here only *once in a while*.

☑ **once upon a time** 從前

Once upon a time there lived a king who
had a gorgeous daughter.

☑ **right away** 立刻 (= *immediately*)

Hearing the news, she hurried home *right
away*.

☑ **so far** 到目前為止

He has read many books *so far*.

☑ **so far as** 就～所及 (= *as far as*)

So far as I can remember, there was a
drugstore opposite the convenience store.

☐ **so long as** 只要 (= *as long as*)

So long as the methods are correct, the ability to read English is not difficult to cultivate.

☐ **sooner or later** 遲早

Sooner or later he will succeed.

☐ **so to speak** 可以說是；好比是

The man is, *so to speak* , a grown-up child.

☐ **straight away** 立刻 (= *right away*)

Would you like some champagne, or do you want dinner *straight away*?

☐ **that is to say** 也就是說 (= *that is*)

He will arrive here next Friday, *that is to say*, the 18th of July.

☐ **then and there** 當場立刻 (= *right then*)

He made up his mind *then and there*.

☐ **the other way around** 恰好相反

I was accused of cheating him of his money but in fact it was *the other way around*.

☐ **to a degree** 有點；有幾分 (= *somewhat*)

Although I tried my best to explain to him, he was, *to a degree*, disinclined to believe me.

☐ **to a great extent** 大大地；非常

Market penetration depends *to a great extent* on the ability of a company to establish a good sales network.

☐ **to a man** 全體一致 (= *unanimously*)

In the meeting all of the directors approved of the company's new policy. They agreed *to a man*.

☐ **to and fro** 來回地 (= *back and forth*)

The man walked *to and fro* while waiting for his bus.

Check List

- [ ] to a man _____
- [ ] once in a blue moon _____
- [ ] once in a while _____
- [ ] so far as _____
- [ ] so long as _____

- [ ] to a degree _____
- [ ] to a great extent _____
- [ ] the other way around _____
- [ ] straight away _____
- [ ] once upon a time _____

- [ ] on trial _____
- [ ] once and for all _____
- [ ] right away _____
- [ ] then and there _____
- [ ] sooner or later _____

📖 同義成語

1. **on time** 準時
   = on the dot
   = on the nose
   = on the button
   = punctually

2. **once and for all**
   = for the last time
   最後一次

3. **right away**
   = straight away
   = at once
   = in a jiffy
   = in an instant
   = in a minute
   = without delay
   = immediately
   立刻

4. **once in a blue moon**
   = almost never
   = very rarely
   = very seldom
   極少有

5. **so to speak**
   = so to say
   = as it were
   可以說是

6. **to a man**
   = without exception
   = with one accord
   = of one accord
   = unanimously
   全體一致

★ STEP 8 ★

☐ **to be frank** 坦白說

To be frank, I don't like your new hat.

☐ **to begin with** 首先；第一點

We can't go. *To begin with*, it's too cold.
Besides, we're busy.

☐ **to be on the safe side** 為了安穩起見；以防萬一（= *just in case*）

Though Miami is rarely crowded during
the summer months, we decided to call for
a hotel reservation *to be on the safe side*.

☐ **to crown it all** 最糟的是

He had his wallet picked and his ID stolen.
To crown it all, his car was towed away.

□ **to make matters worse** 更糟的是

Our teacher wants us to write a ten-page paper. *To make matters worse*, he wants it next week.

□ **to** *one's* **advantage** 對某人有利

No matter what career you choose in the future, it is *to your advantage* to have a good command of English.

□ **to** *one's* **heart's content** 盡情地

I'm starving. Let's eat. I'll eat *to my heart's content*.

□ **to** *one's* **surprise** 令某人驚訝的是

To my surprise, they offered me the job.

□ **to some extent** 在某種程度上；多少

We were lucky *to some extent* because one of our major competitors went out of business.

☐ **to the full** 充分地

Thomas used his abilities *to the full* in this project. He did a wonderful job.

☐ **to the letter** 嚴格地；徹底地

John always does what he is told to do *to the letter*.

☐ **under no circumstances** 絕不

Under no circumstances will I accept a paper given to me after the deadline has passed.

☐ **up and down** 上上下下；到處

When the landlord opened the door, he looked me *up and down* before asking who I was.

☐ **upside down** 上下顛倒地；混亂地

The boy pretended he could read, but he was holding the book *upside down*.

☐ **what is more** 此外 (= *besides*)

These shoes are expensive, and *what is more*, they are too small.

☐ **what we call** 所謂的

He is *what we call* a little prince.

☐ **with folded arms** 雙臂交叉於胸前

Instead of intervening in the fight between those two guys, he looked on *with folded arms*.

☐ **without delay** 立刻 (= *immediately*)

The first-aid measure should be performed *without delay*.

☐ **without fail** 一定

I'll be there at two o'clock *without fail*. See you then.

🏛 Check List

- [ ] to *one's* advantage _____
- [ ] to the full _____
- [ ] upside down _____
- [ ] without fail _____
- [ ] what is more _____

- [ ] to the letter _____
- [ ] to crown it all _____
- [ ] to some extent _____
- [ ] up and down _____
- [ ] what we call _____

- [ ] with folded arms _____
- [ ] to begin with _____
- [ ] without delay _____
- [ ] to *one's* surprise _____
- [ ] to be frank _____

同義成語

1. *to be frank* 坦白說
   = to be frank with you
   = frankly speaking

2. *to begin with*
   = in the first place
   = first of all
   = firstly
   = first
   首先；第一點

3. *to make matters worse*
   = what is worse
   更糟的是

4. *to the letter*
   = exactly
   = precisely
   嚴格地；徹底地

5. *under no circumstances*
   = on no account
   = by no means
   絕不

6. *what is more*
   = moreover
   = furthermore
   = in addition
   = besides
   此外

7. *what we call*
   = what is called
   = so-called
   所謂的

8. *without fail*
   = certainly
   = surely 一定

PART 2 ▶ 動詞用法的成語

⋯ ✦ STEP ⑨ ✦ ⋯

☐ **abide by** 遵守 (= *follow*)

He is a man of his word.　When he makes a promise, he will definitely *abide by* it.

☐ **absent** *oneself* **from** 缺席

He *absented himself from* class yesterday.

☐ **account for** 說明；解釋 (= *explain*)

Such reasoning can hardly *account for* the fact that collecting is often an irrational passion.

☐ **acquaint** *oneself* **with** 熟悉

You should *acquaint yourself with* the facts before you make a decision.

☐ **act upon** （藥）對～有效

The ointment *acts upon* eczema and athlete's foot.

☐ **adapt** *oneself* **to** 適應

Tom found it difficult to *adapt himself to* the new surroundings.

☐ **add fuel to the flames** 火上加油

Cut it out, Jerry. You're not trying to comfort her but are *adding fuel to the flames*.

☐ **add up to** 總計達；等於

All the information we have collected in relation to that case *adds up to* very little.

☐ **agree to** 同意（某事）

I was unwilling to *agree to* the proposal, but it seemed that I had no choice.

☐ **agree with** 同意（某人）

She *agreed with* him about the holiday plan.

☐ **aim at** 以～為目標；瞄準

What are you *aiming at* with this proposal?

☐ **amount to** 總計；共計

John's total income didn't *amount to* more than a few hundred dollars.

☐ **answer for** 為～負責

He failed to carry out the contract, and now he has to *answer for* the failure.

☐ **appeal to** 吸引（= *attract*）

Mary enjoyed the exhibition, but the paintings did not *appeal to* me.

☑ **apply to**　適用於

These rules *apply to* everybody alike.

☑ **ask after**　問候

He *asked after* his sick friend in hospital.

☑ **ask for it**　自討苦吃

I don't want to listen to your complaints.
You *asked for it*.

☑ **attach to**　黏貼；附著

He *attached* the photo *to* the application
form.

☑ **attend to**　注意

The audience in the hall seemed to *attend
to* his speech.

☑ **attribute A to B**　把 A 歸因於 B

He *attributed* his success *to* his mother.

🏛 Check List

☐ act upon _____

☐ acquaint *oneself* with _____

☐ appeal to _____

☐ attend to _____

☐ ask after _____

☐ aim at _____

☐ adapt *oneself* to _____

☐ abide by _____

☐ agree with _____

☐ apply to _____

☐ attribute A to B _____

☐ ask for it _____

☐ amount to _____

☐ absent *oneself* from _____

☐ account for _____

📖 同義成語

1. *abide by*　遵守
   = comply with
   = conform to
   = stick to
   = adhere to
   = observe
   = follow
   = obey

2. *acquaint* oneself
   with
   = be acquainted
   with
   熟悉

3. *adapt* oneself *to*
   = be adapted to
   = be accustomed to
   適應

4. *add up to*
   = amount to
   總計達；等於

5. *answer for*
   = be accountable
   for
   = be responsible
   for
   為…負責

6. *apply to*　適用於
   = be true of

7. *attribute* A *to* B
   = ascribe A to B
   = owe A to B
   把 A 歸因於 B

···• **STEP 10** •···

☐ **back up** 支持

John is upset with me because I didn't
back him *up* when he complained about
our poor work environment. He feels
like I betrayed him.

☐ **based on** 以…為基礎

The relationship between husband and
wife is *based on* mutual trust.

☐ **be absorbed in** 專心於

I *was* so *absorbed in* reading the novel
that I didn't hear someone knocking
at the door.

☐ **be addicted to** 沉迷於；對…上癮

His son *is addicted to* reading detective
stories.

☐ **bear…in mind** 將…牢記在心
(= *keep…in mind*)

It's a good idea. I'll *bear* it *in mind*.

☐ **be at a loss** 茫然；窮於（辭令）

When he called me a thief, I was so indignant that I *was at a loss* for words.

☐ **beat about the bush** 拐彎抹角
(= *beat around the bush*)

Stop *beating about the bush* and tell us the outcome of the speech contest.

☐ **be at home in** 精通 (= *be good at*)

You had better ask the opinion of someone who *is at home in* the subject.

☐ **be bathed in**　籠罩在…當中

Seen in the distance, the cottage *was bathed in* the golden splendor of the setting sun.

☐ **be becoming to**　適合；和…相配

That type of dress *is* very *becoming to* her. It makes her look tall and thin.

☐ **be bent on**　決心；專心於

He *is bent on* entering that prestigious university; therefore, he is studying very hard.

☐ **be bound for**　前往

We're on the wrong train! This train *is bound for* Chicago, not St. Louis.

☐ **be caught in**　遇到（雨、塞車等）

On my way home, I *was caught in* a shower.

☐ **become of** 發生;使遭遇 (= *happen to*)

What will *become of* the children if their father dies?

☐ **be composed of** 由~組成

Water *is composed of* hydrogen and oxygen.

☐ **be conscious of** 知道;察覺到

Being conscious of the danger of it, Martin quit smoking.

☐ **be cut out for** 適合;有做⋯的天賦

John, shy and slow and lazy, doesn't seem to *be cut out for* journalism. He is really not fit for this field.

☐ **be divided into** 被分成

The body of nearly all flowering plants can *be divided into* two systems.

Check List

- [ ] become of _____
- [ ] beat about the bush _____
- [ ] be caught in _____
- [ ] be composed of _____
- [ ] be becoming to _____

- [ ] be absorbed in _____
- [ ] back up _____
- [ ] be at home in _____
- [ ] be bound for _____
- [ ] be cut out for _____

- [ ] be conscious of _____
- [ ] be divided into _____
- [ ] be bent on _____
- [ ] be at a loss _____
- [ ] be bathed in _____

同義成語

1. *back up* 支持
   = stand by
   = side with
   = be on the side of
   = support

2. *be absorbed in*
   = be engrossed in
   = be lost in
   = be devoted to
   = be preoccupied with
   = be bent on
   = concentrate on
   專心於

3. *be composed of*
   = be made up of
   = consist of
   = comprise
   由～組成

4. *be at home in*
   = be adept in
   = be good at
   精通

5. *be bound for* 前往
   = be destined for
   = set out for
   = head for
   = depart for
   = leave for

6. *be conscious of*
   = be aware of
   知道；察覺到

7. *be cut out for*
   = be gifted in
   = have a gift for
   = have a talent for
   適合；有做～的天賦

⋅✦ STEP 11 ✦⋅

☐ **be driving at** 用意所在；打算

I don't like the hints you're dropping about my new hairstyle. What *are* you *driving at*?

☐ **be equal to** 能勝任

I don't think David *is equal to* the work. He is too young.

☑ **be exposed to** 暴露於；接觸

The more one *is exposed to* an English-speaking environment, the better he or she will learn the language.

☐ **be faced with** 面臨；面對 (= *face*)

He *was faced with* a serious problem, but he was sure the he could solve it eventually.

☐ **be famous for** 以~（特點）有名

Switzerland *is famous for* its scenic beauty.

☐ **be fascinated by** 對~著迷

The children *were fascinated by* all the toys in the shop windows.

☐ **be fed up with** 對~受夠了；
對~厭煩

They *were fed up with* her complaints.

☐ **be foreign to** 與~性質相異

Telling a lie *is foreign to* his nature. He is always honest.

☐ **be free from** 沒有；免於

While on vacation, he *was free from* worry.

☐ **be ignorant of**　不知道

His parents *were* kept *ignorant of* the fact that he failed the exam.

☐ **be immune to**　對～免疫

He *is immune to* polio because he has been vaccinated.

☐ **be incapable of**　無法 (= *be unable to*)

It is a mistaken belief that old people *are incapable of* learning anything new at their age.

☐ **be in charge of**　負責

David is the head of the company. He *is in charge of* everything.

☐ **be inclined to**　易於；傾向於

I *'m inclined to* get tired easily.

☐ **be in line with** 與～一致；符合

All of the rules must *be in line with* company policy.

☐ **be junior to** 比～年輕

My younger brother *is* three years *junior to* me.

☐ **belong to** 屬於

As a writer, he really *belongs to* the eighteenth century.

☐ **be made into** 被製成

Strawberries *are* often *made into* jam.

☐ **be native to** 原產於

The koala eats only the leaves of certain eucalyptus trees that *are native to* Australia.

🏛 Check List

☐ be exposed to _____

☐ be foreign to _____

☐ be incapable of _____

☐ be native to _____

☐ be in line with _____

☐ be in charge of _____

☐ be free from _____

☐ be famous for _____

☐ be fed up with _____

☐ be fascinated by _____

☐ be inclined to _____

☐ belong to _____

☐ be faced with _____

☐ be junior to _____

☐ be ignorant of _____

同義成語

1. *be faced with*
   = be confronted with
   = face
   面臨；面對

2. *be famous for*
   = be known for
   = be well-known for
   = be noted for
   = be renowned for
   以～（特點）有名

3. *be in line with*
   = be in accord with
   = be in keeping with
   = agree with
   與～一致；符合

4. *be equal to*
   = be competent for
   = be qualified for
   能勝任

5. *be fed up with*
   = be bored with
   = be sick of
   = be tired of
   = be weary of
   對～厭煩

6. *be inclined to*
   = be prone to
   = be apt to
   = be liable to
   = tend to
   易於；傾向於

┈• **STEP 12** •┈

☐ **be obliged to**　不得不；必須

He *was obliged to* do the work in place of his sick colleague.

☐ **be on good terms with**　和～關係好

I*'m* not *on* very *good terms with* her at the moment.

☐ **be opposed to**　反對

Because her parents didn't like him, they *were opposed to* his marriage proposal.

☐ **be out of touch with** *sb*.
與某人失去聯絡

Two years ago John went abroad for advanced studies and hasn't written us once. So we *are out of touch with him* now.

☐ **be packed with**　擠滿了

Because of the college football game, it was hard to find a place to eat that *wasn't packed with* students.

☐ **be particular about**　講究

She *is particular about* what she wears. She pays much attention to her image.

☐ **be peculiar to**　是～特有的

The chair has a style *peculiar to* the seventeenth century.

☐ **be qualified for**　有資格做

It will be two years before he *is qualified for* that post.

☐ **be referred to as**　被稱為

California *is referred to as* the "Golden State."

☑ **be regarded as** 被認為是

He *was regarded as* the greatest musician of his day.

☑ **be related to** 與～有關

Physics *is* closely *related to* mathematics.

☑ **be responsible for** 是～的原因；
必須對～負責

The earthquake *was responsible for* more than 2,000 deaths.

☑ **be subject to** 須服從～；易遭受～

We *are subject to* the laws of our country.

☑ **be superior to** 優於；比～好

Nobody *is superior to* him in math. He gets the highest scores in class.

☐ **be up to** 由~決定

You can either punish him or let him off.
It *is up to* you.

☐ **be used to + V-ing** 習慣於

I shall probably oversleep as I *am* not
used to getting up early.

☐ **beware of** 當心；提防

When you are on a crowded bus, *beware
of* pickpockets.

☐ **be weary of** 對~厭煩 (= *be tired of*)

I *am weary of* the long spell of rain.

☐ **be worthy of** 值得

His courage *is worthy of* praise.

📖 Check List

☐ be particular about _____

☐ be responsible for _____

☐ be regarded as _____

☐ be weary of _____

☐ be used to + V-ing _____

☐ be up to _____

☐ beware of _____

☐ be obliged to _____

☐ be related to _____

☐ be on good terms with _____

☐ be subject to _____

☐ be peculiar to _____

☐ be packed with _____

☐ be qualified for _____

☐ be superior to _____

📖 同義成語

1. *be obliged to*
   = be required to
   = be supposed to
   = be bound to
   = have to
   = must
   不得不；必須

2. *be opposed to*
   = oppose *oneself* to
   = oppose
   = object to
   = be against
   反對

3. *be packed with*
   = be crowded with
   = be filled with
   = be full of
   擠滿了

4. *be regarded as*
   = be thought of as
   = be looked upon as
   = be thought (to be)
   = be considered
     (to be)
   被認為是

5. *be related to*
   = have something
     to do with
   = be concerned with
   = be connected with
   與～有關

6. *be used to + V-ing*
   = be accustomed
     to + V-ing
   = be in the habit
     of + V-ing
   習慣於

⋯ STEP 13 ⋯

☐ **bite off** 咬下

Don't *bite off* more than you can chew.

☐ **black out** 昏倒（= *faint* ）

John *blacked out* because he didn't eat breakfast, but he woke up a few minutes later.

☐ **blow** *one's* **top** 生氣；發脾氣

Whenever he *blows his top*, he will shout at the top of his voice.

☐ **blow up** 炸毀

To stop the enemy from attacking, the general commanded the soldiers to *blow up* the bridge.

☐ **brace up** 振作精神

The coach encouraged his team to *brace up* after they lost the game.

☐ **break away** 脫離

More than two hundred years ago the United States *broke away* from the British Empire and became an independent country.

☐ **break down** 故障

Our car *broke down* on our way home. We had to call the emergency road service.

☐ **break even** 不賺也不賠；不分勝負

Since I sold the car for exactly what I paid for it, I *broke even* on the deal.

☐ **break into** 闖入

Burglars *broke into* Miss Chen's house last night while she was visiting a friend.

☐ **break loose** 逃脫 (= *escape*)

A criminal *broke loose* from the prison and now the police are looking for him everywhere.

☐ **break off** 中斷 (= *cut off*)

He had to *break off* in the middle of his speech because of the protest from the audience.

☐ **break out** (火災、戰爭、疾病)爆發

A fire *broke out* in the boiler room on account of negligence.

☐ **break the ice** 打破僵局；打破冷場

Our hostess *broke the ice* the moment she began to serve the refreshments.

☐ **break through** 突破；穿過

Thieves *broke through* a wall and a steel partition to get at the safe.

☐ **break up** 分手；(婚姻) 破裂

I haven't seen Peter since he *broke up* with his girlfriend, but I heard he's much more upset about it than she is.

☐ **bring about** 導致 (= *lead to*)

The disagreement about the boundaries between the two countries *brought about* endless war.

Check List

- [ ] break out _____
- [ ] break up _____
- [ ] break into _____
- [ ] break off _____
- [ ] brace up _____
- [ ] break down _____
- [ ] blow *one's* top _____
- [ ] bite off _____
- [ ] black out _____
- [ ] break away _____

- [ ] break loose _____
- [ ] bring about _____
- [ ] blow up _____
- [ ] break the ice _____
- [ ] bring about _____

📖 同義成語

1. **blow** one's **top**
   = hit the ceiling
   = lose one's
     temper
   = fly into a rage
   = fly into a temper
   = get mad
   = see red
   = become angry
   生氣；發脾氣

2. **brace up**
   = perk up
   = cheer up
   振作精神

3. **break down** 故障
   = be out of order
   = be out of
     condition
   = be on the blink

4. **break off** 中斷
   = cut off
   = terminate

5. **break out** 發生
   = spring up
   = come about
   = come to pass
   = take place
   = occur
   = happen

6. **bring about** 導致
   = bring on
   = bring to pass
   = lead to
   = give rise to
   = result in
   = end in
   = cause

⋯ ✦ STEP 14 ✦ ⋯

☐ **bring back** 歸還（ = *return* ）

If you don't like it when you get home, you can always *bring* it *back*.

☐ **bring in** 賺進

The sales of the company's new product are overwhelmingly good. It has *brought in* two million dollars so far.

☐ **bring out** 發揮；顯示

Don't worry about your grades. Just concentrate on your studies. Hard work often *brings out* the best in you.

☐ **bring** *sb*. **to** 使某人甦醒

Helen fainted but the nurse gave her something which *brought her to*.

☐ **bring up** 撫養長大 (= *raise*)

Since he was an orphan, he was *brought up* by his aunt and uncle.

☐ **brush up on** 溫習 (= *review*)

She spent the summer *brushing up on* her Taiwanese history as she was to teach that in the fall.

☐ **build castles in the air** 做白日夢

He likes to *build castles in the air*, but never succeeds in anything.

☐ **build up** 加強

Jack is trying to *build up* his strength again after the illness.

☐ **burn up** 燒光；燒盡

The house *burned up* before the firemen came.

☐ **burst into** 突然（哭、笑）起來

As the clown got into his stride, the audience *burst into* laughter.

☐ **burst out + V-ing** 突然（哭、笑）起來

The girl *burst out crying* when she heard the sad news.

☐ **bury** *one's* **head in the sand**
逃避現實

You can't always *bury your head in the sand*. You should learn to face the music.

☐ **call a spade a spade** 有話直說

The old man hates long and fancy words—he always *calls a spade a spade*.

☐ **call at** 拜訪（某地）

I shall *call at* his house tomorrow.

☐ **call** *sb.* **down** 責罵某人 (= *scold sb.*)

Mother *called* Bob *down* for walking into the kitchen with muddy boots.

☐ **call for** 需要 (= *require*)

The construction of a house *calls for* a lot of money.

☐ **call it a day** 今天到此為止

The four golfers played nine holes and then *called it a day*.

☐ **call it quits** 到此為止

We've worked on the project since morning. I can't keep my eyes open. Let's *call it quits*.

☐ **call off** 取消 (= *cancel*)

The baseball game was *called off* on account of rain.

🏛 Check List

☐ call off

☐ call down

☐ call a spade a spade

☐ brush up on

☐ bring out

☐ bring in

☐ call at

☐ call for

☐ call it quits

☐ burn up

☐ bring to

☐ bring up

☐ build up

☐ burst out + V-ing

☐ call it a day

同義成語

1. *bring sb. to*
   = bring *sb.* around
   = revive *sb.*
   使某人甦醒

2. *brush up on* 溫習
   = review
   = go over
   = look over
   = run over

3. *build castles in the air* 做白日夢
   = build castles in Spain
   = daydream

4. *call a spade a spade* 有話直說
   = call *one's* shot
   = be frank

5. *call sb. down*
   = call *sb.* names
   = call *sb.* on the carpet
   = reprove *sb.*
   = rebuke *sb.*
   = reprimand *sb.*
   = blame *sb.*
   = scold *sb.*
   責罵某人

6. *call for* 需要
   = require
   = need

7. *call it a day*
   = call it quits
   = stop for the day
   = quit
   今天到此為止

⋯ **STEP 15** ⋯

☐ **call on** 拜訪（某人）；呼籲

Mr. Brown *called on* an old friend while he was in the city.

☐ **call** *sb*. **up** 打電話給某人

I hardly knew the man. I couldn't believe it when he *called me up* to chat.

☐ **call** *sth*. **into question**
對某事提出疑問

The scientist's plan to build a modern laboratory was *called into question* on account of its huge budget.

☐ **call upon** 呼籲；要求（= *call on*）

The president is *calling upon* the whole nation to stay rational and calm, lest schism and hatred should arise.

☐ **cannot do without** 不能沒有

In studying English, I just *cannot do without* a dictionary. I need one very much.

☐ **cannot help + V-ing** 忍不住；不得不

As she spoke rather loudly, I *could not help overhearing* what she said.

☐ **carry on with** 繼續

After a short break, they *carried on with* their work.

☐ **care for** 喜歡

I don't really *care for* tea; I like coffee better.

☐ **carry out** 實行；執行

The scientists *carried out* long and complicated star counts over several years.

☐ **cast a spell over** 對~施魔咒；使著迷

The beauty of the tropical islands *cast a spell over* the tourists; they were all fascinated by the view there.

☐ **catch a glimpse of** 匆匆看一眼

At last he stopped before an old house, and *caught a glimpse of* the town.

☐ **catch fire** 著火

When he dropped a match in the leaves, they *caught fire*.

☐ **catch hold of** 抓住

Catch hold of this rope, and try to climb up the cliff.

☐ **catch on** 流行；受歡迎

The new style seems to have *caught on* this year.

☐ **catch** *one's* **breath** 喘一口氣；
休息一下

After running to the bus stop, we sat
down to *catch our breath*.

☐ **catch on to** 了解 (= *understand*)

I was surprised at how quickly Lydia
caught on to computer programming.

☐ **catch sight of** 看到

My friend greeted me as soon as he
caught sight of me.

☐ **catch some Z's** 小睡片刻

I feel so tired. I want to hit the sack and
catch some Z's.

☐ **catch the point** 了解

I'm sorry, but I didn't *catch the point*.
Can you say that again?

🏛 Check List

- [ ] catch *one's* breath _____
- [ ] call upon _____
- [ ] call *sb.* up _____
- [ ] catch a glimpse of _____
- [ ] cast a spell over _____

- [ ] catch the point _____
- [ ] cannot do without _____
- [ ] catch sight of _____
- [ ] catch some Z's _____
- [ ] carry on with _____

- [ ] carry out _____
- [ ] catch on _____
- [ ] catch on to _____
- [ ] catch hold of _____
- [ ] call *sth.* into question _____

同義成語

1. *call sb. up*
 = make a phone call to sb.
 = give sb. a call
 = give sb. a ring
 = give sb. a buzz
 = telephone sb.
 = phone sb.
 = call sb.
 打電話給某人

2. *call upon*
 = call on
 = appeal to
 = require
 呼籲；要求

3. *carry out* 實行
 = put…into practice
 = put…into effect
 = put…into force

4. *cannot do without*
 = cannot dispense with 不能沒有

5. *cannot help* + *V-ing*
 = cannot help but + V.
 = cannot but + V.
 忍不住；不得不

6. *catch hold of*
 = take hold of
 = grab hold of
 = grasp
 抓住

7. *catch on to* 了解
 = figure out
 = make out
 = understand

⋯•★ STEP 16 ★•⋯

☐ **catch up with** 趕上

Though he started the class three weeks late, he works hard to *catch up with* the others.

☐ **center on** 集中於；指向（= *focus on*）

Speculation about a series of terrorist attacks *centered on* Saudi dissident Osama Bin Laden.

☐ **change for the better** 好轉

The position of women has definitely *changed for the better* over the years.

☐ **cheer up** 激勵；鼓舞

The support of the students *cheered up* the losing team and they played harder and won.

☑ **clean up** 清理

Who's going to *clean up* all this mess?

☑ **cling to** 緊抓不放

At the party we saw that shy girl *clinging to* her mother all the time.

☑ **clutch at** 緊抓

A drowning man will *clutch at* a straw.

☑ **come about** 發生 (= *happen*)

Nobody saw how the accident *came about*.

☑ **come across** 偶然看見

One day I *came across* a newspaper article about the retirement of a professor at a nearby state college.

☑ **come across** 偶然遇到

To my surprise, I *came across* an old friend at the railway station yesterday.

☑ **come by** 獲得 (= *obtain*)

I am curious about how John *came by* such a large sum of money.

☑ **come down with** 因～而病倒；罹患

She *came down with* pneumonia last month.

☑ **come in** 有 (尺寸、顏色、形狀等)

These nails *come in* three standard sizes.

☑ **come into existence** 產生；形成

It is said that the universe *came into existence* of itself.

☑ **come into sight** 出現 (= *appear*)

After we had been on the ocean for ten days, land *came into sight*.

☑ **come near to** 幾乎

The failure of the company *came near to* ruining him.

☑ **come out** 出版；出現

His new novel will *come out* next month.

☑ **come to** 甦醒 (= *revive*)

After artificial respiration was performed, the drowning man finally *came to*.

☑ **come to an end** 結束；終止

The discussion *came to an end* after all the members reached an agreement.

🏛 Check List

- ☐ change for the better _____
- ☐ clean up _____
- ☐ come across _____
- ☐ come into sight _____
- ☐ come to an end _____

- ☐ come into existence _____
- ☐ cheer up _____
- ☐ center on _____
- ☐ come about _____
- ☐ come in _____

- ☐ come to _____
- ☐ come out _____
- ☐ come down with _____
- ☐ clutch at _____
- ☐ catch up with _____

同義成語

1. catch up with
   = come up with
   = keep up with
   = keep abreast of
   趕上；與…並駕齊驅

2. come about
   = come off
   = come to pass
   = break out
   = spring up
   = take place
   = happen
   = occur
   發生

3. come across
   = run across
   = run into
   = bump into
   偶然遇到

4. come to
   = come to *oneself*
   = come to *one's* senses
   = revive
   甦醒

5. come by 獲得
   = acquire
   = obtain
   = get

6. come down with
   = become sick with
   = catch
   罹患

7. come to an end
   = cease
   = stop
   結束；終止

⋯•★ STEP 17 ★•⋯

☐ **come to** *one's* **senses** 甦醒

The boxer was knocked out and didn't *come to his senses* for several minutes.

☐ **come to** *oneself* 恢復知覺

It was a long time before he *came to himself*.

☐ **come to pass** 發生 (= *happen*)

I will see that such a thing does not *come to pass*.

☐ **come to terms** 達成協議

The boys argued over whether to play baseball or football but finally *came to terms* by voting to play baseball.

☑ **come true** 實現

He works so hard that I believe his dream will *come true* some day.

☐ **come up** 出現

Many problems *come up* when students go abroad to study.

☐ **come up against** 面臨；碰到

No matter how tough the difficulty they *come up against*, they are determined to face and solve it.

☐ **come up to** 符合 (=*meet*)；來到…身邊

The concert was an excellent one. It *came up to* our expectations.

☐ **come up with** 想出；提出

I couldn't *come up with* an excuse when my teacher asked me why I was late.

☐ **come what may**　無論發生什麼事

Come what may, I shall always love her.

☐ **commit suicide**　自殺

He failed in his attempt to *commit suicide* because he was sent to the hospital in time.

☐ **compare A to B**　把 A 比喻為 B

We often *compare* life *to* a journey.

☐ **compensate for**　彌補（= *make up for*）

Nothing can *compensate for* the loss of one's health.

☐ **comply with**　遵守（= *obey*）

All of us should *comply with* rules and laws.

☐ **confine** *oneself* **to**　侷限於

I will *confine myself to* making a few
remarks.

☐ **congratulate** *sb.* **on~**　恭喜某人~

He *congratulated* me *on* successfully
passing the entrance exam.

☐ **consist in**　在於（= *lie in*）

The beauty of this picture *consists in* its
balance of colors.

☐ **consist of**　由~組成

A football team *consists of* eleven players
on offense and eleven players on defense.

☐ **contribute to**　促成；有助於；導致

The construction of a highway will
contribute to the growth of the suburbs.

🏛 Check List

- ☐ come to terms _____
- ☐ come to pass _____
- ☐ commit suicide _____
- ☐ come up to _____
- ☐ come up with _____

- ☐ compare A to B _____
- ☐ compensate for _____
- ☐ contribute to _____
- ☐ come to *oneself* _____
- ☐ come up against _____

- ☐ consist of _____
- ☐ come what may _____
- ☐ comply with _____
- ☐ confine *oneself* to _____
- ☐ consist in _____

同義成語

1. **come to terms**
   = come to an agreement
   = make terms
   達成協議

2. **commit suicide**
   = do *oneself* in
   = take *one's* own life
   = kill *oneself*
   自殺

3. **comply with** 遵守
   = abide by
   = observe
   = follow
   = obey

4. **come what may**
   = whatever may come
   = whatever happens
   = at any rate
   = in any case
   = anyway
   無論發生什麼事

5. **consist of**
   = comprise
   = be made up of
   = be composed of
   由～組成

∗ STEP 18 ∗

☐ **convince A of B** 使 A 相信 B

He tried in vain to *convince* them *of* his innocence.

☐ **cool down** 冷卻

As the weather in Taiwan is *cooling down*, Taipei residents are heading for hot springs to refresh themselves.

☐ **cop out** 中途退縮；逃避

He promised to help me with my homework but *copped out* at the last minute.

☐ **cope with** 應付

The death of her parents is very sad, but it's something she will have to *cope with*.

☐ **correspond to** 和～一致；符合

In the English language, sounds do not always *correspond to* a letter.

☐ **correspond with** 與（某人）通信

I often *correspond with* my friends in America.

☐ **count on** 依賴；指望

The company was *counting on* Brown's making the right decision.

☐ **cover up** 掩蓋；掩飾

The newspapers printed the story before the government could *cover* it *up*.

☐ **crack down on** 嚴格取締

The police plan to *crack down on* the selling of liquor to minors.

☐ **crash into** 猛然撞上

The car *crashed into* a tree and burst into flames.

☐ **cut corners** 走捷徑;抄近路

He *cut corners* in order to get the work done quickly.

☐ **cut down on** 減少 (= *reduce*)

You had better budget your money and *cut down on* unnecessary expenses.

☐ **cut in** 打斷 (= *interrupt*)

I hate it when someone *cuts in* while I am talking.

☐ **cut it out** 住嘴

Just *cut it out*! I've had enough of your silly jokes.

☐ **cut off**　切斷

The electricity to our house was *cut off* yesterday because we hadn't paid the bill for three months.

☐ **cut** *sb.* **short**　打斷（某人的話）

Brian was about to announce our plan but I *cut him short*.

☐ **cut short**　中斷；提前結束

The meeting was *cut short* by the announcement of a fire. All the people were evacuated from the building.

☐ **date from**　可追溯至；始於

The custom *dates from* the time when men wore swords.

🏛 Check List

- ☐ convince A of B _____
- ☐ cut off _____
- ☐ cut it out _____
- ☐ date from _____
- ☐ cut corners _____

- ☐ correspond with _____
- ☐ correspond to _____
- ☐ cool down _____
- ☐ cop out _____
- ☐ crack down on _____

- ☐ cut down on _____
- ☐ cut short _____
- ☐ cope with _____
- ☐ count on _____
- ☐ cut in _____

同義成語

1. cop out
   = back out
   = hold back
   中途退縮

2. cope with
   = deal with
   = contend with
   應付

3. cut corners
   = take a shortcut
   抄捷徑；走近路

4. correspond to
   = be agreeable to
   = be in conformity
     with
   和…一致；符合

5. count on
   = rely on
   = depend on
   = trust
   依賴；指望

6. date from
   = date back to
   = can be traced
     back to
   可追溯至

⋯⋆ STEP ⑲ ⋆⋯

☐ **deal with** 與～有關

One of Einstein's most important works is Special Relativity, which *deals with* high-speed motion.

☐ **deal with** 應付；處理 (= *cope with*)

As a general manager, you need to know how to *deal with* your subordinates effectively.

☐ **depend on** 視～而定；依賴

Prices of vegetables vary greatly *depending on* the season.

☐ **derive from** 源自

These English words *derive from* French.

☐ **devote** *oneself* **to** 致力於

He intends to *devote himself to* curing the sick in Africa.

☐ **die away** 漸漸消失；漸漸減弱

The sound of the train gradually *died away*.

☐ **die down** 逐漸消失；靜下來

As the applause *died down*, the curtain on the stage dropped slowly.

☐ **die out** 滅絕

This bird is in danger of *dying out*.

☐ **dispense with** 免除；不用

(= *do without*)

In our high technology-oriented society, we can't *dispense with* computers.

☐ **dispose of** 處理 (= *deal with*)

We ought to be able to *dispose of* the business in one hour.

☐ **dispose of** 處理掉；清除 (= *get rid of*)

We have *disposed of* all our old clothes by donating them to a charity organization.

☐ **do a snow job on** *sb.* 欺騙某人

I suspected that they were trying to *do a snow job on me*, so I didn't accept their offer.

☐ **do away with** 廢除 (= *abolish*)

We have to *do away with* the old system before adopting the new one.

☐ **do credit to** 替某人增光

This book will *do credit to* the author.

☑ **do harm to** 對…有害

Most people know that smoking will *do harm to* their health.

☑ **do** *sb.* **good** 對某人有益

It will *do you good* to take some time off.

☑ **do the sights of** 參觀（某地）

Three days is very little time to *do* all *the sights of* London.

☑ **do without** 將就不用

I cannot afford a car, so I'll just have to *do without*.

☑ **dress up** 盛裝打扮

Are we going to *dress up* for the party, or is it informal?

🏛 Check List

☐ depend on _____

☐ dispose of _____

☐ do away with _____

☐ die out _____

☐ do the sights of _____

☐ die away _____

☐ die down _____

☐ do harm to _____

☐ do *sb.* good _____

☐ deal with _____

☐ do a snow job on _____

☐ dress up _____

☐ do credit to _____

☐ dispense with _____

☐ devote *oneself* to _____

📖 同義成語

1. *deal with*
   = be concerned with
   = be about
   與～有關

2. *do a snow job on* sb.
   = pull sth. on sb.
   = put sth. over on sb.
   = lead sb. on
   = take sb. in
   = deceive sb.
   = cheat sb.
   欺騙某人

3. *derive from*
   = be derived from
   = originate from
   = have one's origin from
   = come from
   源自

4. *devote oneself to*
   = be devoted to
   = commit oneself to
   = be committed to
   = dedicate oneself to
   = be dedicated to
   致力於

5. *do away with*
   = put an end to
   = abolish 廢除

···* STEP 20 *···

☐ **drag down** 拖垮

Nobody knows when the shaky financial system will *drag down* the economy of this country.

☐ **draw near** （時間）接近；快要到了

The time is *drawing near* when Mary will have to leave for school.

☐ **draw the line** 劃清界線；使有區別

We should *draw the line* between public and private affairs.

☐ **draw up** 草擬

He helped the company *draw up* a blueprint for how to resolve the many problems facing the company now.

☐ **drop by** 順道拜訪

I am glad to have you *drop by*.

☐ **drop in on** *sb.* 順道拜訪某人

When Tina was visiting San Diego, she decided to *drop in on* her aunt, who lives there.

☐ **drop out** 輟學

She left school before graduating. In other words, she *dropped out*.

☐ **drop** *sb.* **a line** 寫信給某人

I decided to *drop her a line* since I hadn't heard from her for a long time.

☐ **dwell on** 談論；老是想著

The speaker *dwelt on* the difficulties of teaching in college.

☐ **earn a living** 謀生

He found it difficult to *earn a living* only by writing.

☐ **end up** 結果

He *ended up* failing the test because he did not study hard enough for it.

☐ **face the music** 接受處罰；承擔後果

You messed up everything in the living room. When Mom comes home, you'll have to *face the music*.

☐ **fall behind** 落後

France had *fallen behind* Britain and Germany in automobile production, and it had slumped into fourth place in aircraft manufacturing.

☐ **fall in with** 符合

The idea they put to us *fell in* exactly *with* what we ourselves had in mind.

☐ **fall off** 減少 (= *decrease*)

Their sales *fell off* sharply when the war broke out.

☐ **fall on** （節日）適逢（星期幾）

Christmas *fell on* a Sunday last year.

☐ **fall short of** 未達到；不足

The results of the examination *fell short of* the teacher's expectations.

☐ **fall through** 失敗；無法實現

His plan to go abroad for advanced studies *fell through* because his father fell sick suddenly.

🏛 Check List

☐ earn a living   _____

☐ drop by   _____

☐ drop in on *sb.*   _____

☐ fall in with   _____

☐ fall off   _____

☐ drag down   _____

☐ dwell on   _____

☐ end up   _____

☐ draw near   _____

☐ fall short of   _____

☐ fall behind   _____

☐ drop out   _____

☐ draw up   _____

☐ draw the line   _____

☐ face the music   _____

同義成語

1. draw near
   = draw on
   = be near at hand
   = be around the
     corner
   接近;快要到了

2. draw up 草擬
   = make a draft of
   = draft
   = compose

3. drop in on sb.
   = look in on sb.
   = run in to see sb.
   = pay a casual
     visit to sb.
   順道拜訪某人

4. drop sb. a line
   = write sb. a note
   = write sb. a letter
   = write to sb.
   寫信給某人

5. dwell on
   = speak a lot about
   = think a lot about
   談論;老是想著

6. earn a living
   = make a living
   謀生

7. fall through
   = come to nothing
   = fail
   失敗;無法實現

··· ★ STEP 21 ★ ···

☐ **figure out** 了解 (= *understand*)

Sam couldn't *figure out* how to print out the document until the teacher showed him.

☐ **fill out** 填寫 (= *fill in*)

When you apply for your passport, you have to *fill out* many different forms.

☐ **fill** *sb.* **in** 告訴某人

Whenever I have any questions, my father always *fills* me *in*.

☐ **find fault with** 挑剔

She tries to please him, but he always *finds fault with* everything she does.

☐ **find shelter** 躲避

Due to the strong sun, many people *found shelter* under the large tree.

☐ **fire away** 開始說話、發問

I am in a hurry so if you want to ask any questions, *fire away*.

☐ **flatter** *oneself* 自以為

He *flatters himself* that he is the best speaker of English.

☐ **fly into a rage** 生氣；大發雷霆

After he learned that his best friend had sold him out, he *flew into a rage*.

☐ **follow suit** 仿效；跟著別人的樣子做

When our competitor started offering a 20% discount, we had no choice but to *follow suit* and reduce our prices as well.

☐ **fool around**　鬼混；游手好閒

He spends so much time *fooling around* that he never accomplishes anything.

☐ **gear up**　使準備好；使躍躍欲試

After the coach's pep talk, our team was all *geared up* to go out and win the championship game.

☐ **get across to**　被～理解

The teacher tried to explain the problem, but the explanation did not *get across to* the class.

☐ **get along**　進展

Frank is *getting along* in France better than he expected.

☐ **get away with** 逃避處罰

With the teacher around, how did he *get away with* cheating on the examination?

☐ **get carried away** 激動 (= *get excited*)

She *got* so *carried away* when arguing with her husband that she burst into tears.

☐ **get cold feet** 怯場

He was going to ask Jane to dance with him but he *got cold feet* and didn't.

☐ **get even with** 報復

He betrayed me, so I have made up my mind to *get even with* him some day.

☐ **get going** 開始做

The foreman told the workmen to *get going*.

🏛 Check List

☐ fill out　　　　　　＿＿＿＿＿

☐ flatter *oneself*　　＿＿＿＿＿

☐ get across to　　　＿＿＿＿＿

☐ get cold feet　　　＿＿＿＿＿

☐ figure out　　　　＿＿＿＿＿

☐ fool around　　　＿＿＿＿＿

☐ find shelter　　　＿＿＿＿＿

☐ follow suit　　　　＿＿＿＿＿

☐ get away with　　＿＿＿＿＿

☐ get going　　　　＿＿＿＿＿

☐ get even with　　＿＿＿＿＿

☐ get along　　　　＿＿＿＿＿

☐ fly into a rage　　＿＿＿＿＿

☐ find fault with　　＿＿＿＿＿

☐ fill *sb.* in　　　　＿＿＿＿＿

同義成語

1. *fly into a rage*
   = lose *one's* temper
   = blow up
   = blow *one's* top
   = hit the ceiling
   = hit the roof
   = get mad
   = see red
   = take offense
   = become angry
   生氣；大發雷霆

2. *figure out* 了解
   = make out
   = get on to
   = catch on to
   = make sense of
   = understand

3. *fool around*
   = hang around
   = mess around
   = goof around
   = play around
   鬼混；游手好閒

4. *get even with*
   = get back at
   = have revenge on
   = take revenge on
   = be revenged on
   = revenge *oneself* on
   報復

5. *find shelter*
   = take shelter
   = find protection
   躲避

⋯ ★ STEP 22 ★ ⋯

☐ **get hold of**　找到（＝*find*）

At last we *got hold of* our friend after
trying to telephone many times.

☐ **get in the way**　擋路

The police asked the bystanders to move
over and not to *get in the way* when the
firefighters came to the rescue.

☐ **get in touch with**　與～聯絡

Tina wants to *get in touch with* her teacher,
whom she hasn't seen for a long time.

☐ **get into scrapes**　惹上麻煩；陷入困境

He didn't take his parents' advice and
soon *got into* all kinds of *scrapes*.

□ **get into the swing of things**
適應情況

I've only been at work for a week, so I haven't *got into the swing of things* yet.

□ **get it over with** 做完

This assignment is very boring. I want to *get it over with* as soon as possible.

□ **get off** 下車

Be sure to take the No.2 bus, and *get off* at 21st street.

□ **get on** 上（飛機、車、船）(= *board*)

Fortunately John arrived at the airport and *got on* the plane in time.

□ **get on** *one's* **nerves** 使某人心煩

That noise *gets on my nerves*. Will you please turn down the volume?

☑ **get** *one's* **own way**　為所欲為

I can't just let my children *get their own way*. Spare the rod and spoil the child.

☑ **get over**　克服；自～中恢復

Peter's sudden death was a great blow to Jane and it took her a long time to *get over* the grief.

☑ **get rid of**　除去；擺脫

If you *get rid of* all that junk, you will have much more room.

☑ **get the upper hand over**
比～佔優勢；比～佔上風

In the third round, the champion *got the upper hand over* his opponent and knocked him out.

☐ **get through** 完成 (= *finish*)

I didn't *get through* studying last night until almost eleven o'clock.

☐ **get used to** 習慣於

People traveling abroad always have to *get used to* new food.

☐ **give a big hand** 鼓掌 (= *applaud*)

The audience *gave a big hand* to the soloist for his outstanding performance.

☐ **give away** 捐贈；贈送

Rockefeller was a great philanthropist. He *gave away* millions.

☐ **give birth to** 生 (小孩) (= *bear*)

I heard my neighbor's cat *gave birth to* five kittens.

🏛 Check List

- [ ] get in the way _____
- [ ] get *one's* own way _____
- [ ] get rid of _____
- [ ] get on *one's* nerves _____
- [ ] get through _____

- [ ] get on _____
- [ ] get off _____
- [ ] get over _____
- [ ] get through _____
- [ ] get the upper hand _____

- [ ] get it over with _____
- [ ] get in touch with _____
- [ ] give birth to _____
- [ ] get used to _____
- [ ] get hold of _____

🔖 同義成語

1. **get in touch with**
   = get in contact with
   = communicate with
   = contact
   與～聯絡

2. **get one's own way**
   = have one's own way
   = do as one wishes
   為所欲為

3. **get rid of**
   = get free from
   = get out of
   = throw off
   = shake off
   除去；擺脫

4. **get the upper hand over**
   = get an advantage over
   = get the better of
   = get the best of
   = get ahead of
   比～佔優勢

5. **get used to**
   = get accustomed to 習慣於

6. **give birth to**
   = be delivered of
   = bear
   生（小孩）

7. **get into scrapes**
   = get into trouble
   陷入困境；惹上麻煩

★ STEP 23 *★*

☐ **give in** 倒塌 (= *collapse*)；屈服

The bridge *gave in* under the weight of
the heavy truck.

☐ **give in to** 向～屈服；向～投降

"It's not our policy to *give in to* the
demands of terrorists," a government
spokesman stressed.

☐ **give it to** *sb.* **straight** 坦白告訴某人

He asked the doctor to *give it to him*
straight how long he would live.

☐ **give off** 散發出 (= *release*)

The gas *gives off* an unpleasant smell.

☐ **give out** 分發 (= *distribute*)；發出

At the graduation ceremony next week, our principal will *give out* diplomas.

☐ **give rise to** 引起；導致 (= *cause*)

John's reckless behavior *gave rise to* endless troubles for his parents.

☐ **give** *sb.* **a ring** 打電話給某人

Give me a ring sometime next week and we'll arrange to have dinner together.

☐ **give up** 放棄 (= *quit*)

You had better *give up* smoking for your own sake.

☐ **give way to** 被～取代

Recently in Taiwan, the manufacturing industry has *given way to* the information industry.

☐ **go all out** 盡全力 (= *try one's best*)

Next year is an election year. The prospective presidential candidates are *going all out* to win the support of people from every walk of life.

☐ **go bananas** 瘋了 (= *go crazy*)

Andy works so hard that he sleeps only about two hours every night. I think he has *gone bananas*.

☐ **go easy on** 溫和地對待

Don't punish the boy severely; *go easy on* him.

☐ **go for** 喜愛；受～吸引

I don't *go for* war films in a big way.

☐ **go from bad to worse**

每下愈況；越來越糟

John's typing *went from bad to worse* when he was tired.

☐ **go halves** 平均分攤；各付各的

That was an expensive meal—let's *go halves*.

☐ **go in for** 喜歡 (= *like*)

Mr. Harrison's wife *goes in for* classical music, while he himself hasn't the slightest interest in it.

☐ **go into** 進入；成爲～狀態

I was almost frightened to death when the plane suddenly *went into* a sharp nosedive.

Check List

- [ ] go in for _____
- [ ] give in _____
- [ ] give off _____
- [ ] go into _____
- [ ] give out _____

- [ ] give way to _____
- [ ] go easy on _____
- [ ] give up _____
- [ ] give rise to _____
- [ ] give it to *sb.* straight _____

- [ ] go halves _____
- [ ] go from bad to worse _____
- [ ] give in to _____
- [ ] give *sb.* a ring _____
- [ ] go bananas _____

同義成語

1. *give in to*
   = give way to
   = yield to
   = surrender to
   = give *oneself* up to
   向～屈服；向～投降

2. *give off* 散發出
   = put forth
   = let out
   = emit

3. *give rise to*
   = lead to
   = bring about
   = bring to pass
   = result in
   = end in
   = cause
   引起；導致

4. *go bananas* 發瘋
   = go nuts
   = go out of *one's* mind
   = become crazy

5. *go in for*
   = care for
   = have a liking for
   = delight in
   = take delight in
   = take to
   = be fond of
   = be crazy about
   = like 喜歡

6. *go halves*
   = go fifty-fifty
   = go Dutch
   平均分攤；各付各的

ᐧᐧᐧᐧᐧ STEP 24 ᐧᐧᐧᐧᐧ

☐ **go into details** 詳細描述

Let's not *go into details*; just keep to the main points.

☐ **go off** （鬧鐘、鈴）開始響；爆炸

Suddenly the fire alarm *went off* and everyone had to leave the building.

☐ **go on** 繼續

The teacher *went on* talking for two hours.

☐ **go out** 熄滅

The light *went out* and we were left in the dark.

☐ **go steady** 穩定交往

At first Tom and Nicole were not serious about each other, but now they are *going steady*.

☐ **go through** 經歷

You will never know what she *went through* in order to raise her children.

☐ **go to any lengths** 竭盡所能

A drug addict will *go to any lengths* to obtain his drugs.

☐ **go with** 配合 (= *match*)

The necklace she bought yesterday *went well with* her earrings.

☐ **goof off** 偷懶；混日子

The employees would *goof off* when the boss wasn't around.

☐ **grow out of** 長大後戒除（壞習慣）

He has *grown out of* the bad habits of his boyhood days and is now a mature youngster.

☐ **hand in** 繳交（= *submit*）

All students are supposed to *hand in* their reports by the end of the month.

☐ **hand over** 交給；移交

He *handed over* the keys of the office to the police.

☐ **hang on** 堅持（= *persevere*）

If all the manufacturers can *hang on* during this financial crisis, the economy may get better next quarter.

☐ **hang on to** 保住；緊握

I'd *hang on to* that house for the time being; house prices are rising sharply at the moment.

☐ **hang out** 逗留

Many young people like to *hang out* with friends in nightclubs or Internet cafés.

☐ **happen to + V.** 碰巧

They *happened to* see her coming across the street.

☐ **have a bone to pick with** *sb.*
挑剔某人；對某人不滿

I don't like the teacher because he always *has a bone to pick with me*.

🏛 Check List

☐ hang out　　　　　_____

☐ hang on to　　　　_____

☐ happen to + V.　_____

☐ go steady　　　　_____

☐ goof off　　　　　_____

☐ hand over　　　　_____

☐ go with　　　　　_____

☐ hand in　　　　　_____

☐ go out　　　　　_____

☐ go to any lengths　_____

☐ go off　　　　　　_____

☐ hang on　　　　　_____

☐ grow out of　　　_____

☐ go on　　　　　　_____

☐ go into details　　_____

同義成語

1. **go off**
   = begin to ring
   = begin to buzz
   開始響

2. **go on**
   = continue with
   = persevere with
   繼續

3. **go to any lengths**
   = go to great
     lengths
   = go to considerable
     lengths
   = do anything *one*
     can
   竭盡所能

4. **go out**
   = blow out
   = be put out
   = be extinguished
   熄滅

5. **hand in**
   = turn in
   = submit
   繳交

6. **go through**
   = suffer
   = experience
   經歷

⋯⋆ STEP 25 ⋆⋯

☐ **have a crush on** 迷戀；愛上

As a big fan of Brad Pitt, Sue regards him as her prince charming. She *has a crush on* him.

☐ **have a good command of** 精通

My secretary *has a good command of* English.

☐ **have a say in** 有發言權

Every member of the group *has a say in* how things should be done, That is to say, everyone has some influence on the decision.

☐ **have a voice in** 有發言權；參與

Women should *have a voice in* our society rather than play their traditional roles.

☑ **have charge of** 負責

Mary *has charge of* all the arrangements for the party.

☑ **have enough of** 受夠了；厭煩

I have *had enough of* his nonsense.

☑ **have eyes in the back of** *one's* **head** 注意一切而不動聲色

Mother must *have eyes in the back of her head*, because she always knows when I do something wrong.

☑ **have it in for** 對～懷恨在心

The teacher has *had it in for* John ever since the time that he insulted her in front of the class.

☐ **have nothing in common**
沒有共同點

Jane and Sue are twins, but they seem to
have nothing in common.

☐ **have** *one's* **hands full**　忙得不可開交

With small children and a lot of household
chores to take care of, Mary *has her hands
full.*

☐ **have** *one's* **heart set on**　想要；希望

For years he *had his heart set on* purchasing
a house of his own.

☐ **have words with**　和～爭吵

I *had words with* the saleswoman at that
department store because she refused to
refund my money for a compact disc
player that wasn't operating properly.

☐ **have something to do with**
和～有關

Satisfaction and happiness *have something to do with* income.

☐ **head for** 前往 (= *start for*)

In the fall many birds *head for* the south.

☐ **heap praise upon** 對～大加稱讚

Though her parents *heap praise upon* her musical ability, Jenny's piano playing is really terrible.

☐ **hear from** 接到消息；收到～的信

He hasn't been *heard from* since he left the country.

☐ **hear of** 聽說 (= *hear about*)

We asked many people about the restaurant, but no one had *heard of* it.

🏛 Check List

- [ ] have charge of _____
- [ ] have a say in _____
- [ ] have enough of _____
- [ ] have nothing in common

  _____
- [ ] have it in for _____
- [ ] hear of _____
- [ ] have a voice in _____
- [ ] have words with _____
- [ ] have a crush on *sb.* _____
- [ ] have *one's* hands full _____
- [ ] have…to do with _____
- [ ] head for _____
- [ ] hear from _____
- [ ] have *one's* heart set on _____
- [ ] heap praise on _____

同義成語

1. *have a crush on*
   = be stuck on
   = be attracted to
   迷戀；愛上

2. *have a good command of*
   = be master of
   = be at home in
   = be proficient in
   = be expert in
   = be adept in
   = be good at 精通

3. *have something to do with*
   = be related to
   = be connected with
   = be concerned with 和~有關

4. *have one's heart set on* 渴望
   = set *one's* heart upon
   = be anxious for
   = long for
   = crave
   = desire

5. *have it in for*
   = hold a grudge against
   對~懷恨在心

6. *have words with*
   = have a quarrel with
   = be at odds with
   = argue with
   = quarrel with
   和~爭吵

⋯⋆ STEP 26 ⋆⋯

☐ **hit on** 想到 (= *hit upon*)

I *hit on* the solution to the problem.

☐ **hit the ceiling** 非常生氣

When Mary came home at three in the morning, her father *hit the ceiling*. He was furious.

☐ **hit the mark** 命中目標；成功

A fool's bolt may sometimes *hit the mark*.

☐ **hit the road** 上路；出發

It's getting late. It's time for us to *hit the road*.

☐ **hit upon** 偶然發現；偶然遇到

We *hit upon* a new road back to town while we were out for a ride last Sunday.

□ **hold back** 抑制；忍住

Seeing me stumble over her legs, Tracy fought hard to *hold back* her laughter.

□ **hold good** 適用；有效

The basic design of the miniskirt has *held good* for more than 25 years.

□ **hold on** 堅持；(電話) 不掛斷

They managed to *hold on* until help arrived.

□ **hold on to** 緊握 (= *grasp*)

I *held on to* my little brother's hand in the crowd lest he get lost.

□ **hold** *one's* **breath** 屏氣凝神

The people all *held their breath* and listened to the announcement.

□ **hold** *one's* **horses**　稍安勿躁

The professor asked us to *hold our horses* until he had finished the class.

□ **hold** *one's* **tongue**　保持沉默

If people would *hold their tongues* when they want to say something unkind, fewer people would be hurt.

□ **hold up**　使延誤（ = *delay* ）

I was *held up* by a traffic jam on the freeway for about an hour.

□ **hold up**　搶劫（ = *rob* ）

They not only *held up* the owner of the stall but also hurt him badly.

□ **hold with**　同意；贊成（ = *agree* ）

I don't *hold with* his pessimistic views.

☐ **identify with** 認同；支持

Many teenagers in Taiwan tend to *identify with* Japanese pop singers, no matter how weird they look.

☐ **immerse** *oneself* **in** 埋首於；專心於

The scholar tried to strike up a conversation; the man, however, continued to *immerse himself in* his book.

☐ **insist on** 堅持（ = *persist in* ）

They *insisted on* my taking the golden opportunity.

☐ **jump to conclusions** 遽下結論

Don't *jump to conclusions*, for it's easy to cause misunderstandings.

🏛 Check List

☐ hold with _____

☐ hit on _____

☐ identify with _____

☐ hit the ceiling _____

☐ hit the mark _____

☐ hit the road _____

☐ hold good _____

☐ hold on _____

☐ hold on to _____

☐ hold *one's* tongue _____

☐ hold up _____

☐ hold *one's* breath _____

☐ hit upon _____

☐ immerse *oneself* in _____

☐ jump to conclusions _____

同義成語

1. sb. **hit on** sth.
   = sb. hit upon sth.
   = sb. think of sth.

   = sth. occur to sb.
   = sth. strike sb.

   某人想到某事

2. **hit the ceiling**
   = blow one's top
   = lose one's temper
   = fly into a rage

   = see red
   = go crazy
   = become angry

   非常生氣

3. **hold** one's **tongue**
   = hold one's peace

   = keep quiet
   = say nothing

   保持沉默

4. **hold back**
   = keep back

   = restrain
   = control

   抑制；忍住

5. **hold with**
   = agree with (sb.)

   = agree to (sth.)
   = be agreeable to

   = assent to
   = consent to
   = be favorable to

   = approve of
   = be in favor of
   = be on the side of

   = be for
   = approve

   贊成；同意

⋯⋆ STEP 27 ⋆⋯

☐ **keep abreast of**　跟上；不落後

Doctors should *keep abreast of* all the latest developments in medicine.

☐ **keep an eye on**　注意；監視

That man looks suspicious. *Keep an eye on* him.

☐ **keep back**　遠離

After the accident, the police told the crowd to *keep back*.

☐ **keep down**　壓制（＝ *repress*）

The people have been *kept down* for years by a brutal regime, which totally controls the police and military.

☐ **keep from** 避免 (= *avoid*)

Take lots of vitamin C to *keep from* catching a cold.

☐ **keep good hours** 早睡早起

Keeping good hours makes you healthy.

☐ **keep…in mind** 記住 (= *remember*)

You should *keep in mind* that he is not as strong as he used to be.

☐ **keep it up** 繼續努力

You will have to *keep it up* if you want to swim faster than other swimmers in our country.

☐ **keep off** 和…保持距離

The notice in the park said "*Keep off* the grass."

☐ **keep on** 繼續（＝ *continue*）

They *kept on* listening to the radio until three o'clock in the morning.

☐ **keep** *one's* **composure** 保持鎮定

A true sportsman *keeps his composure* even when he is losing.

☐ **keep** *one's* **head above water** 保持收支平衡

Joseph's income declined so drastically that he had difficulty *keeping his head above water*.

☐ **keep out** 勿接近；保持距離

There is a sign on the front door which says, "Dog inside, *keep out*."

☐ **keep pace with** 跟上

When they go for a walk, Johnny has to take long steps to *keep pace with* his father.

☐ **keep** *sb.* **in suspense**
使某人懸疑緊張

The mystery thriller *kept* the audience *in suspense* until the secret was revealed at the end of the movie.

☐ **keep** *sth.* **under** *one's* **hat** 保守秘密

Mr. Wilson knew who had won the contest, but he *kept it under his hat* until it was announced publicly.

☐ **keep to** *oneself* 不與人交往

George doesn't mix much; he likes to *keep to himself*.

🏛 Check List

☐ keep off　　　　　　＿＿＿＿＿＿

☐ keep down　　　　　　＿＿＿＿＿＿

☐ keep to *oneself*　　　＿＿＿＿＿＿

☐ keep pace with　　　　＿＿＿＿＿＿

☐ keep out　　　　　　＿＿＿＿＿＿

☐ keep *sb.* in suspense　＿＿＿＿＿＿

☐ keep from　　　　　　＿＿＿＿＿＿

☐ keep on　　　　　　　＿＿＿＿＿＿

☐ keep good hours　　　＿＿＿＿＿＿

☐ keep abreast of　　　　＿＿＿＿＿＿

☐ keep back　　　　　　＿＿＿＿＿＿

☐ keep *one's* composure　＿＿＿＿＿＿

☐ keep an eye on　　　　＿＿＿＿＿＿

☐ keep···in mind　　　　＿＿＿＿＿＿

☐ keep it up　　　　　　＿＿＿＿＿＿

同義成語

1. *keep abreast of*
   = remain abreast of
   = keep step with
   = keep pace with
   = keep up with
   = catch up with
   跟上；不落後

2. *keep an eye on*
   = have an eye on
   = keep *one's* eye on
   = have *one's* eye on
   = keep watch on
   = watch
   注意；監視

3. *keep good hours*
   = keep early hours
   早睡早起

4. *keep…in mind*
   = bear…in mind
   = have…in mind
   = commit…to memory
   = learn…by heart
   記住

5. *keep sth. under one's hat*
   = keep *sth.* dark
   = keep *sth.* to *oneself*
   = keep *sth.* a secret
   = make a secret of *sth.*
   保守秘密

⚡ STEP 28 ⚡

☐ **keep track of** 知道；與⋯保持聯繫

We should read the newspaper to *keep track of* the events happening in the world every day.

☐ **keep track of** 記錄

You must *keep track of* all your expenses while you are traveling abroad.

☐ **keep up with** 跟上

We learn as much as possible for fear that we might not *keep up with* the times.

☐ **kick the habit** 戒掉壞習慣

He has long been addicted to alcohol, even though he has tried to *kick the habit* of drinking.

☐ **kill time**　打發時間；消磨時間

Many people play mahjong because they simply don't have other ways of *killing time*.

☐ **knock it off**　停止；不要吵

Mother told my little brother to *knock it off* when he was being naughty.

☐ **know** *sb.* **by sight**　認得某人

I *know him by sight* but I have never actually spoken to him.

☐ **lay aside**　儲蓄

Mary planned to buy a new bicycle, so she *laid aside* a few dollars each week.

☐ **lay down**　放下（ = *put down* ）

The police persuaded the hijacker to *lay down* his weapons and release the hostages.

☐ **lay off** 解僱（ = *fire* ）

Because of the recession, many small companies had to *lay off* a large number of their workers.

☐ **lead to** 導致；造成（ = *result in* ）

Unemployment often *leads to* lots of social problems, including a higher crime rate.

☐ **learn⋯by heart** 記住

The teacher wanted us to *learn* Lincoln's Gettysburg speech *by heart*.

☐ **leave⋯behind** 忘了攜帶；留下

Some passengers' packages were *left behind* on the buses.

☐ **leave off** 停止 (= *stop*)

"I'd like to start from where we *left off* yesterday. Please turn to page 120 in your textbooks."

☐ **leave out** 刪掉 (= *omit*)

The writer was upset because the editor *left out* a large and important part of his story.

☐ **let off** 從輕發落；放～一馬

The mother said she would *let off* her son from washing the dishes if he could finish his assignment before supper.

☐ **let on** 洩露（秘密）(= *reveal*)

He asked me not to *let on* to Jenny that we were planning a secret birthday party for her.

Check List

- ☐ learn…by heart
- ☐ lay aside
- ☐ keep up with
- ☐ leave off
- ☐ keep track of

- ☐ know *sb.* by sight
- ☐ lead to
- ☐ lay off
- ☐ knock it off
- ☐ let on

- ☐ lay down
- ☐ kill time
- ☐ leave…behind
- ☐ leave out
- ☐ kick the habit

📑 同義成語

1. *keep track of*
   = keep in touch
     with
   = be in touch with
   = be in contact with
   與…保持聯繫

2. *keep track of*
   = keep tabs on
   = keep a record of
   記錄

3. *knock it off*
   = cut it out
   = lay off
   = stop
   停止；不要吵

4. *lay aside* 儲蓄
   = put aside
   = set aside
   = lay by
   = put by
   = put away
   = salt away
   = store up
   = save

5. *lead to* 導致
   = give rise to
   = bring about
   = bring on
   = bring to pass
   = result in
   = end in
   = cause

⟪ STEP 29 ⟫

□ **let out** 洩露

Don't you ever *let out* our plan to anyone.
You hear me?

□ **let** *sb.* **down** 使某人失望

You can always rely on people like Ann.
They never *let you down*.

□ **let up** 減緩；停止

I'm afraid the game has to be called off.
The rain shows no sign of *letting up*.

□ **lie in** 在於 (= *consist in*)

My friend believes that the greatest
happiness *lies in* freedom from worldly
cares.

☑ **light up** 照亮

After the invention of electricity, lanterns were no longer used to *light up* the house at night.

☑ **live by** 按照～標準生活

Because we are afraid that we might look different from others, we *live by* the norms of the society we live in.

☑ **live from hand to mouth** 僅夠溫飽

Refugees in that camp have been *living from hand to mouth* for two months.

☑ **live it up** 狂歡

Thank God it's Friday! Let's go to a KTV to *live it up*.

□ **live on** 以～為食；繼續活著

In the Philippines, fishermen raise fish in underwater cages, and the fish *live on* a diet of bran and ice cream cones.

□ **live up to** 達成

Tom works very hard, but he still doesn't *live up to* his parents' expectations.

□ **look after** 目送 (= *follow with the eye*)

Mike *looked after* his father with a gloomy look until he was out of sight.

□ **look after** 照顧 (= *take care of*)

Mr. Newman hired a baby-sitter to *look after* his baby girl while he and his wife went out to dinner.

☐ **look back on** 回顧

The day she got married is a day she will always *look back on* with happiness.

☐ **look down upon** 輕視

We shouldn't *look down upon* others just because they were born to poor families.

☐ **look forward to** 期待

How excellent it feels to *look forward to* a holiday!

☐ **look into** 調查 (= *investigate*)

After a series of robberies, the police decided to *look into* the break-ins thoroughly.

☐ **look out for** 注意 (= *watch out for*)

Drivers must *look out for* children crossing the road.

🏛 Check List

- [ ] let *sb*. down _____
- [ ] look out for _____
- [ ] lie in _____
- [ ] live it up _____
- [ ] let up _____

- [ ] look back on _____
- [ ] light up _____
- [ ] live on _____
- [ ] look into _____
- [ ] let out _____

- [ ] live by _____
- [ ] live up to _____
- [ ] look after _____
- [ ] look down upon _____
- [ ] look forward to _____

同義成語

1. *look into*
   = investigate
   = inspect
   = examine
   調查

2. *look down upon*
   = sneeze at
   = make light of
   = make little of
   = think little of
   = think nothing of
   = think scorn of
   = feel scorn for
   = be scornful of
   = scorn
   = despise
   輕視

3. *look after*
   = see after
   = take care of
   = care for
   = attend to
   = watch over
   = keep an eye on
   照顧

4. *look forward to*
   = anticipate
   期待

5. *look out for*
   = watch out for
   = be alert for
   注意

⋅ STEP 30 ⋅

☑ **look out on** 瀕臨；面臨（= face）

I would like a room *looking out on* the sea.

☑ **look over** 看過一遍（= review）

The manager *looked over* all the papers the secretary gave him.

☑ **look over** 檢查（= examine）

I suggest that you *look over* these figures before you submit them in your final report.

☑ **look up** 好轉；抬頭看

Last year was tough, but our business is beginning to *look up*.

☐ **look up to** 尊敬（= *respect*）

A man who has done such a heroic deed should be *looked up to* by everyone.

☐ **lose faith of** 對⋯失去信心

Jim completely *lost faith of* his ability when his team was beaten in the soccer tournament.

☐ **lose** *one's* **temper** 發脾氣

I tried to be calm but finally I *lost my temper*.

☐ **lose track of** 和⋯失去聯絡

We haven't seen John for a long time. As a matter of fact, we have *lost track of* him.

☐ **make a fool of** 愚弄；使出醜

If you dress like that at your age, you'll *make a fool of* yourself.

□ **make a mockery of**
使…顯得荒謬或無價值

The unfair and hasty decision of the court *made a mockery of* the trial.

□ **make a nuisance of** *oneself*
使自己惹人討厭

He has *made a nuisance of himself* by buttonholing anyone he could to ask a question.

□ **make a reservation**　預訂

It is always a good idea to *make a reservation* far in advance if you are planning to stay in a hotel on Waikiki Beach during the summer vacation.

□ **make allowances for**　考慮；體諒

The boy had certainly done wrong, but his father *made allowances for* his youth.

□ **make believe** 假裝 (= *pretend*)

I *made believe* that I was enthusiastic so as not to disappoint her.

□ **make every effort** 盡力

I will *make every effort* to reach my goal.

□ **make faces** 扮鬼臉

The naughty boy *made faces* at the teacher when he was not being observed.

□ **make for** 有助於；走向

I hope that this decision will *make for* friendly relations between the two countries.

□ **make no difference** 沒有差別

It *makes no difference* which road you take; both lead to the station and they are equally long.

🏛 Check List

☐ make no difference　＿＿＿＿＿＿

☐ make for　＿＿＿＿＿＿

☐ lose faith of　＿＿＿＿＿＿

☐ make a mockery of　＿＿＿＿＿＿

☐ make believe　＿＿＿＿＿＿

☐ look over　＿＿＿＿＿＿

☐ lose *one's* temper　＿＿＿＿＿＿

☐ make faces　＿＿＿＿＿＿

☐ make allowances for　＿＿＿＿＿＿

☐ look up　＿＿＿＿＿＿

☐ lose track of　＿＿＿＿＿＿

☐ make a reservation　＿＿＿＿＿＿

☐ make every effort　＿＿＿＿＿＿

☐ look up to　＿＿＿＿＿＿

☐ make a fool of　＿＿＿＿＿＿

同義成語

1. look up to
   = have a regard for
   = be respectful of
   = respect
   尊敬

2. lose track of
   = lose contact with
   和…失去聯絡

3. make believe
   = make as if
   = make as though
   = make out as
     though
   = pretend
   假裝

4. make allowances
   for
   = allow for
   = take…into
     account
   = take…into
     consideration
   = take account of
   = consider
   考慮；體諒

5. make every effort
   = make an effort
   = make efforts
   盡力

✦ STEP ㉛ ✦

☐ **make nothing of** 不在乎；忽視

Making nothing of the cold, he went out in a thin shirt.

☐ **make off** 逃走（= *escape*）

I tried to stop her but she *made off* in a hurry.

☐ **make out** （勉強地）看出；辨認出

"Can you *make out* what the sign says?"
"Yes.　From where I'm standing it's quite clear.　It says, 'No Smoking.'"

☐ **make something of** 認爲某事不尋常

I wonder if Peter *made something of* what I told him.

☐ **make the most of** 善用

The government should face up to the situation and try to *make the most of* it.

☐ **make up** 和好 (= *end a quarrel*)；編造

Don't worry too much. This couple often argue but they will *make up* soon.

☐ **make up** 編造

Irene is a very lazy girl. She always *makes up* excuses to avoid household chores.

☐ **make up for** 彌補 (= *compensate for*)

Her intelligence *made up for* her lack of personal charm.

☐ **make up** *one's* **mind** 下定決心

I have *made up my mind* about what to major in when I go to college.

☐ **make way** 讓路

Those people in front of the door, please *make way* for others.

☐ **meet** *sb.* **halfway** 與某人妥協

At last her father *met her halfway* and agreed to let her go out.

☐ **mix up** 使混淆 (= *confuse*)

Instead of helping me, his explanation only *mixed* me *up*.

☐ **occur to** 想到

It never *occurred to* me that I should bump into an old classmate at the airport.

☐ **part company with** 與～意見不合

On that question I am afraid I must *part company with* you.

☐ **participate in** 參加 (= *take part in*)

I invited my elder brother to *participate in* the meeting.

☐ **pass away** 去世；死亡 (= *die*)

Queen Elizabeth I *passed away* in 1603.

☐ **pass by** 疏忽；置之不理 (= *ignore*)

A good teacher should not *pass by* bad behavior as if it were good.

☐ **pass for** 被認為 (= *be considered*)

She was the type of person who might have *passed for* an actress.

☐ **pass out** 昏倒

On hearing the shocking news, she let out a cry and *passed out*.

🏛 Check List

- ☐ make way　　　＿＿＿＿＿＿＿
- ☐ make nothing of　＿＿＿＿＿＿＿
- ☐ make the most of　＿＿＿＿＿＿＿
- ☐ make up *one's* mind　＿＿＿＿＿＿
- ☐ pass out　　　＿＿＿＿＿＿＿

- ☐ mix up　　　＿＿＿＿＿＿＿
- ☐ make off　　　＿＿＿＿＿＿＿
- ☐ make up　　　＿＿＿＿＿＿＿
- ☐ pass out　　　＿＿＿＿＿＿＿
- ☐ participate in　＿＿＿＿＿＿＿

- ☐ make out　　　＿＿＿＿＿＿＿
- ☐ pass away　　　＿＿＿＿＿＿＿
- ☐ meet *sb*. halfway　＿＿＿＿＿＿
- ☐ make something of　＿＿＿＿＿＿
- ☐ make up for　＿＿＿＿＿＿＿

同義成語

1. **make the most of**
   = make the best of
   = make the best use of
   善用

2. **make up for**
   = make amends for
   = compensate for
   = atone for
   彌補

3. **pass away**
   = pass on
   = be done for
   = be no more
   = kick the bucket
   = turn up *one's* toes
   = meet *one's* death
   = die
   去世；死亡

4. **pass by**
   = pass over
   = pass off
   = push aside
   = brush aside
   = pay no attention to
   = be ignorant of
   = ignore
   忽視

5. **pass for**
   = be regarded as
   = be thought of as
   = be looked upon as
   = be considered (to be)
   = be thought (to be)
   被認為是

···* **STEP 32** *···

☐ **pass the buck** 推卸責任

It's your job to set a date for the promotion, so don't *pass the buck*. Make a decision.

☐ **pay attention to** 注意

You should *pay attention to* even the smallest detail of the report.

☐ **pay for** 爲~付出代價

She will be made to *pay for* her stupidity.

☐ **pay lip service to** *sb.* 敷衍某人

The students all *paid lip service to* the teacher when she told them to work harder. They didn't care a bit about what she said.

☐ **pay off** 還清；有了成果

He planned to *pay off* his loan over ten years.

☐ **pick on** 欺負；選擇

It is not fair to *pick on* kids with disabilities just because they are different.

☐ **pick out** 挑選（= *choose*）

I went to the bookstore to *pick out* a birthday card for a classmate of mine.

☐ **pick up** 學會

It is believed that one can *pick up* a language more quickly in an environment where the language is widely used.

☐ **play a ~ role** 扮演一個~角色

She *plays an* important *role* in the play.

☐ **play down** 低調處理；對～輕描淡寫

They tried hard to *play down* the seriousness of local fights to prevent a large scale war from taking place.

☐ **play it by ear** 見機行事；隨機應變

John wanted to *play it by ear* when he went for his interview, so he didn't prepare for it in advance.

☐ **play up to** 拍馬屁；討好 (= *flatter*)

Students who too obviously *play up to* their teachers are usually disliked by their classmates.

☐ **point at** 指著

It is rude to *point at* people.

☐ **point out** 指出 (= *indicate*)

The teacher *pointed out* the mistakes in my composition.

☐ **pour oil on the fire** 火上加油

Shut up! You are not helping him out. You are just *pouring oil on the fire*.

☐ **prefer A to B** 喜歡 A 甚於 B

I *prefer* going on foot *to* going by bus.

☐ **present A with B** 把 B 送給 A

The company *presented* him *with* a gold watch on the day he retired.

☐ **present** *oneself* 出現；露面

The chairman *presented himself* at the press conference in perfect shape.

🏛 Check List

- ☐ pour oil on the fire _____
- ☐ point at _____
- ☐ pick out _____
- ☐ pay lip service to *sb*. _____
- ☐ pay off _____

- ☐ pass the buck _____
- ☐ play down _____
- ☐ pick up _____
- ☐ present *oneself* _____
- ☐ play up to _____

- ☐ pay attention to _____
- ☐ pick on _____
- ☐ play it by ear _____
- ☐ prefer A to B _____
- ☐ pay for _____

📖 同義成語

1. ⎧ ***pay attention to***
   ⎪ = turn *one's*
   ⎪   attention to
   ⎩ = give attention to
   ⎧ = pay heed to
   ⎪ = give heed to
   ⎩ = attend to
   ⎧ = take notice of
   ⎪ = take note of
   ⎩ = take heed of
   注意

2. ⎧ ***play up to***
   ⎪ = make up to
   ⎩ = shine up to
   ⎧ = butter up
   ⎪ = curry favor with
   ⎩ = lick *one's* boots
   ⎧ = apple-polish
   ⎩ = flatter
   拍馬屁；討好

3. ⎧ ***present*** oneself
   ⎪ = come into sight
   ⎩ = make the scene
   ⎧ = show up
   ⎪ = turn up
   ⎩ = turn out
   ⎧ = make an
   ⎪   appearance
   ⎪ = enter an
   ⎩   appearance
   ⎧ = put in an
   ⎪   appearance
   ⎩ = appear
   出現；露面

⟨ ★ STEP 33 ★ ⟩

☑ **pull down**　拆除

The old houses will soon be *pulled down* and rebuilt because of the severe damage caused by the earthquake.

☑ **pull into**　駛入

The train *pulled into* the station exactly on time.

☑ **pull** *one's* **weight**　盡本分

We can succeed only if everyone on the team *pulls his weight*.

☑ **pull** *oneself* **together**　振作起來

After the failure of his business, he was never able to *pull himself together*.

☐ **pull out** 拔出

I nearly fainted when my dentist told me that he'd have to *pull out* two of my teeth.

☐ **put a period to** 使停止；終止

The suspect's confession *put a period to* the investigation.

☐ **put across** 講明白；說清楚

The idea of a balanced diet is difficult to *put across* to those who know little about food values.

☐ **put an end to** 停止

We must *put an end to* this kind of quarrel.

☐ **put aside** 儲存

Every month Peter *puts* $500 *aside* for any emergency that might arise.

☑ **put away** 收好

Students were told to *put away* their books and take out a piece of paper to have a test.

☑ **put down** 平定；鎮壓 (= *suppress*)

The troops easily *put down* the rebellion.

☑ **put down** 寫下 (= *write down*)

Put the date *down* in your diary so that you won't forget it.

☑ **put forth** 提議；發表

He has *put forth* a new theory of the origin of the solar system. (89 日大)

☑ **put forward** 提出 (計劃) (= *propose*)

If any man here does not agree with me, he should *put forward* his own plan.

☐ **put off** 延期 (= *delay* = *postpone*)

Due to the dense fog, the departure of the airplane was *put off*.

☐ **put on** 裝出

The man *put on* a brave face and accepted the challenge.

☐ **put on an act** 裝模作樣

Richard is far from being rich. He is only *putting on an act*.

☐ **put out** 熄滅 (= *extinguish*)

Would you please *put out* the cigarette? I can't stand the smoke here.

☐ **put** *sb.* **on** 欺騙某人 (= *fool sb.*)

He often tried to *put me on* but I always knew better.

🏛 Check List

- ☐ put an end to　　　　　＿＿＿＿＿＿
- ☐ put down　　　　　　　＿＿＿＿＿＿
- ☐ put on　　　　　　　　＿＿＿＿＿＿
- ☐ put out　　　　　　　　＿＿＿＿＿＿
- ☐ put aside　　　　　　　＿＿＿＿＿＿

- ☐ put forth　　　　　　　＿＿＿＿＿＿
- ☐ put on an act　　　　　＿＿＿＿＿＿
- ☐ pull *one's* weight　　　＿＿＿＿＿＿
- ☐ put a period to　　　　＿＿＿＿＿＿
- ☐ put away　　　　　　　＿＿＿＿＿＿

- ☐ put off　　　　　　　　＿＿＿＿＿＿
- ☐ pull down　　　　　　　＿＿＿＿＿＿
- ☐ put across　　　　　　　＿＿＿＿＿＿
- ☐ put on　　　　　　　　＿＿＿＿＿＿
- ☐ put *sb.* on　　　　　　＿＿＿＿＿＿

📖 同義成語

1. *pull down*
   = tear down
   = demolish
   = destroy
   拆除

2. *pull one's weight*
   = do *one's* part
   = do *one's* full
     share of work
   盡本分

3. *put a period to*
   = put an end to
   = put a stop to
   = bring…to a close
   = bring…to a stop
   = call a halt to
   使停止；終止

4. *put aside*
   = set aside
   = lay aside
   = lay by
   = put by
   = put away
   = salt away
   = save up
   = save
   儲存

5. *put down*
   = take down
   = set down
   = write down
   = make a note of
   = make notes of
   = take a note of
   = take notes of
   寫下；記錄

⋯ STEP 34 ⋯

☐ **put** *sb.* **up**　收留某人

The Wangs had nowhere to go so we *put them up* for the weekend.

☐ **put⋯into practice**　把⋯付諸實行

After you have learned something new, it is important that you try to *put it into practice*.

☐ **put together**　組合（= *assemble*）

When it came to *putting* the model airplane *together*, Tom was the quickest.

☐ **put up**　興建（= *construct*）

They are tearing down that old building in order to *put up* a new one.

☐ **put up with** 忍受 (= *bear*)

Since he was accustomed to having a
room to himself, it was difficult for him
to *put up with* a roommate.

☐ **qualify for** 有…資格

All the seeds *qualified for* the tennis
tournament.

☐ **rain cats and dogs** 下傾盆大雨

It *rained cats and dogs* last night, so we
didn't go to the movies.

☐ **rain out** 因雨取消

It rained heavily yesterday, so the ball
game was *rained out* in the seventh inning.

☐ **reach for** 伸手去拿

She stood on tiptoe and *reached for* the
book on the top shelf.

☐ **react to** 對…有反應 (= *respond to*)

I'm wondering how he will *react to* the news of the team's victory.

☐ **refer to** 提及；引述

He likes to *refer to* the Bible in his speech.

☐ **refrain from** 克制自己不要

Please *refrain from* smoking in public places.

☐ **rely on** 信賴；依賴 (= *count on*)

Don't trust him; he is the last man to *rely on*.

☐ **remind** *sb.* **of** *sth.* 使某人想起某事

This song *reminds* me *of* the good old days.

☐ **resort to** 訴諸於

The President warned that if the enemy did not withdraw their troops, he would have to *resort to* military force.

☐ **result from** 起因於

Many car accidents *result from* drunken driving. I think the government should impose severe punishments on those drunk drivers.

☐ **ride out** 安然度過（= *survive*）

If you can *ride out* this crisis, you will have a good chance of success.

☐ **rise in the world** 功成名就

You will never *rise in the world* without a little more perseverance.

Check List

- [ ] qualify for　　　　　＿＿＿＿＿＿＿
- [ ] reach for　　　　　　＿＿＿＿＿＿＿
- [ ] remind *sb*. of *sth*.　＿＿＿＿＿＿＿
- [ ] rise in the world　　　＿＿＿＿＿＿＿
- [ ] react to　　　　　　　＿＿＿＿＿＿＿

- [ ] resort to　　　　　　＿＿＿＿＿＿＿
- [ ] put together　　　　　＿＿＿＿＿＿＿
- [ ] rain cats and dogs　　＿＿＿＿＿＿＿
- [ ] refer to　　　　　　　＿＿＿＿＿＿＿
- [ ] result from　　　　　＿＿＿＿＿＿＿

- [ ] put up　　　　　　　＿＿＿＿＿＿＿
- [ ] rain out　　　　　　　＿＿＿＿＿＿＿
- [ ] refrain from　　　　　＿＿＿＿＿＿＿
- [ ] ride out　　　　　　　＿＿＿＿＿＿＿
- [ ] put up with　　　　　＿＿＿＿＿＿＿

同義成語

1. *put…into practice*
   = put…into effect
   = put…into force
   = carry…into
     practice
   = carry out
   把…付諸實行

2. *put up with*
   = tolerate
   = endure
   = stand
   = bear
   忍受

3. *refrain from*
   = abstain from
   = keep *oneself*
     from
   克制自己不要

4. *rely on*
   = count on
   = depend on
   信賴；依賴

5. *result from*
   = be caused by
   起因於

⟐ STEP 35 ⟐

☐ **rise to** *one's* **feet** 站起來（= *stand up*）

When the mayor walked into the room, we
all *rose to our feet* to greet him. We gave
him a standing ovation.

☐ **rule out** 排除

The doctor took X-rays to *rule out* the
chance of broken bones.

☐ **run across** 偶然看到；偶然遇到

I *ran across* his telephone number in an
old address book of mine.

☐ **run errands** 跑腿；出差

The manager always asks me to *run
errands* for him during office hours.

☐ **run into** 偶然遇到 (= *come across*)

I'm glad to *run into* you here because I have urgent business to discuss with you.

☐ **run off** 逃走

Adam forgot to close the gate and the dog *ran off*.

☐ **run out of** 用完

We have *run out of* sugar. Go buy some more.

☐ **run over** 複習 (= *review*)；輾過

During the lunch hour, Jane *ran over* her notes so she would remember them for the test.

☐ **rub** *sb*. **the wrong way** 激怒某人

My father's friends called me a little boy, and that *rubbed me the wrong way*.

☑ **screw up**　搞砸；弄糟（= *mess up*）

She had *screwed up* everything and had to do it all over again.

☑ **see** *sb*. **through**　幫助某人度過（難關）

His courage and good humor *saw him through* the hard times.

☑ **see** *sth*. **in perspective**
以正確的眼光看待某事

No matter what happens, we must *see* our life *in perspective*.

☑ **see through**　看穿；識破

I can't understand how your father managed to *see through* that man.　He had deceived all the rest of us.

☑ **send for** *sb*. 請某人來

We must *send for* a mechanic to repair our car at once.

☑ **serve** *one's* **turn** 符合某人的需要

Helen's house collapsed during the massive earthquake. But she is satisfied that the simple shelter can *serve her turn*.

☑ **set about** 開始；著手

Having decided to rent a flat, we *set about* contacting all the accommodation agencies in the city.

☑ **set back** 阻礙；使延誤（= *delay*）

The rain *set back* the building plan by one week.

🏛 Check List

- ☐ screw up _____
- ☐ rule out _____
- ☐ run off _____
- ☐ see *sb.* through _____
- ☐ rub *sb.* the wrong way _____

- ☐ run errands _____
- ☐ run over _____
- ☐ see through _____
- ☐ set back _____
- ☐ run across _____

- ☐ run out of _____
- ☐ see *sth.* in perspective _____
- ☐ set about _____
- ☐ run into _____
- ☐ send for *sb.* _____

📑 同義成語

1. *rise to one's feet*
   = get to *one's* feet
   = stand up
   站起來

2. *run into*
   = bump into
   = come across
   = come upon
   = hit upon
   = chance upon
   = happen to meet
   = meet
     unexpectedly
   偶然遇到

3. *screw up*
   = mess up
   = blow up
   搞砸;弄糟

4. *run over*
   = go over
   = look over
   = brush up on
   = review
   複習

5. *run off*
   = run away
   = take to *one's* heels
   = take wing
   = sneak away
   逃走

6. *rub sb. the wrong way*
   = burn *sb.* up
   = make *sb.* angry
   激怒某人

⋯ * STEP 36 * ⋯

☐ **set fire to** 放火燒

A few burnt matches were found at the scene of the fire, but the police have not found out who *set fire to* the house yet.

☐ **set free** 釋放 (= *release*)

After the war had ended, they *set* all the prisoners *free*.

☐ **set the world on fire** 有成就

Mary has great talent for playing the piano. She could *set the world on fire* with her piano playing.

☐ **set off** 出發

What time are you planning to *set off* tomorrow?

☐ **set out** 出發 (= *set off*)

They *set out* at dawn in accordance with their commander's orders.

☐ **set up** 設立 (= *establish*)

They decided to *set up* a committee to deal with all these matters.

☐ **show off** 炫耀；賣弄

The topic he chose for his talk was designed to *show off* his expertise in machinery.

☐ **show up** 出現 (= *appear*)

Fifteen people *showed up* at the meeting as scheduled.

☐ **shy away from** 躲避；退縮

I've never *shied away from* saying what I believe in.

☐ **sign off** 收播 (↔ *sign on*)

The station *signs off* with the playing of the national anthem.

☐ **sit on the fence** 觀望；猶豫

Peter doesn't know which man he wants to elect chairman; that is, he is still *sitting on the fence*.

☐ **sit up** 熬夜

Mrs. Smith will *sit up* until her daughter comes home.

☐ **sleep late** 起得晚

The novelist used to *sleep late*; he never got up before eleven o'clock in the morning.

☐ **sleep on** 考慮一晚

After *sleeping on* the matter, he decided to study locally, not overseas.

☑ **slip** *one's* **mind** 被某人遺忘

Sorry! What you said the other day has *slipped my mind*. Would you mind repeating it for me?

☑ **smell out** 嗅出；探聽出

We tried every possible means to *smell out* the secret, but to no purpose.

☑ **spare no expense** 不惜一切花費

He *spared no expense* to make the party a success.

☑ **speak highly of** 讚揚

Both teachers and students *speak highly of* Maggie, the model student of the year.

☑ **speak ill of** 說…的壞話

We should not *speak ill of* others behind their backs.

🏛 Check List

- ☐ set free   _____
- ☐ set out   _____
- ☐ show up   _____
- ☐ sleep late   _____
- ☐ set the world on fire   _____

- ☐ set up   _____
- ☐ shy away from   _____
- ☐ sleep on   _____
- ☐ set off   _____
- ☐ sign off   _____

- ☐ slip *one's* mind   _____
- ☐ set fire to   _____
- ☐ show off   _____
- ☐ sit on the fence   _____
- ☐ smell out   _____

同義成語

1. *set free* 釋放
   = let go
   = let off
   = release

2. *set out* 出發
   = set off
   = set forth

3. *show up* 出現
   = turn up
   = turn out
   = come into sight
   = present *oneself*
   = make an
     appearance
   = enter an
     appearance
   = put in an
     appearance
   = appear

4. *shy away from*
   = fight shy of
   = steer clear of
   = give…a wide
     berth
   = avoid
   躲避

5. *sit up* 熬夜
   = stay up
   = burn the
     midnight oil

6. *speak highly of*
   = speak well of
   讚揚

7. *speak ill of*
   = speak evil of
   = speak badly of
   說…的壞話

⟨∗ STEP 37 ∗⟩

☐ **specialize in**　專攻；主修（= *major in*）

John will *specialize in* applied physics
next year.

☐ **stand by**　支持（= *support*）

John used to *stand by* me whenever I was
in trouble.

☐ **stand for**　代表（= *represent*）

One of the most popular and exciting
sports in the United States is scuba diving.
Scuba *stands for* "self-contained
underwater breathing apparatus."

☐ **stand out**　傑出；突出

His works *stand out* from other novels.
He is an excellent writer.

☐ **stand out against** 抵抗

We managed to *stand out against* all attempts to close the company down.

☐ **stand up for** 維護

The workers protested before the gate of the factory in order to *stand up for* the rights they deserved.

☐ **stand up to** 對抗

It was brave of her to *stand up to* those bullies.

☐ **stay out of** 遠離 (= *keep away from*)

John tried to *stay out of* trouble, but it was impossible for him.

☐ **step down**　辭職；下台（ = *resign* ）

The public asked the Minister of National
Defense to *step down* to take responsibility
for the accident.

☐ **stick to**　堅持；信守

Because Edgar was convinced of the
accuracy of this fact, he *stuck to* his
opinion.

☐ **stir up**　煽動；鼓勵

The coach's pep talk *stirred up* the team
enough to win.

☐ **strike a balance**　（兩者間）取得平衡

It is hard for a country to *strike a balance*
between economic development and
environmental protection.

☐ **strike home** 正中要點

I could see from her expression that his sarcastic comments had really *struck home*.

☐ **strike up** 開始

Peter likes to talk and can *strike up* a conversation with anybody.

☐ **submit to** 向…屈服

He *submitted to* the temptation and stole the wallet.

☐ **succeed to** 繼承

The eldest son *succeeded to* all the property.

☐ **take a fancy to** 喜歡

He bought the house because his wife *took a fancy to* it.

📖 Check List

- ☐ take a fancy to _____
- ☐ stand for _____
- ☐ stand up to _____
- ☐ stir up _____
- ☐ succeed to _____

- ☐ stand out _____
- ☐ stay out of _____
- ☐ strike a balance _____
- ☐ specialize in _____
- ☐ stand out against _____

- ☐ step down _____
- ☐ strike home _____
- ☐ submit to _____
- ☐ stand by _____
- ☐ stand up for _____

📖 同義成語

1.
┌ ***stand by***
└ = stick by
┌ = back up
│ = side with
└ = be on the side of
┌ = stick up for
│ = stand up for
└ = come out for
┌ = take part with
│ = take the part of
│ = take sides with
└ = support

支持

2.
┌ ***take a fancy to***
└ = have a fancy for
┌ = take a liking to
└ = have a liking for
┌ = delight in
│ = take delight in
└ = be crazy about
┌ = care for
└ = go in for
┌ = take to
│ = be fond of
└ = like

喜歡

⋯⋆ STEP 38 ⋆⋯

☐ **take account of** 考慮到

If you *take account of* the fact that she only started learning French last year, she speaks the language very well.

☐ **take advantage of** 利用

We ought to *take advantage of* this opportunity to strengthen the economy of our country.

☐ **take after** 相像 (= *resemble*)

He *takes after* his father both in his appearance and in his character.

☐ **take apart** 拆開

Let's *take* the radio *apart* to see what's wrong with it.

☐ **take care of** 照顧

Helen will *take care of* the baby while we are at the movies.

☐ **take charge** 接管;負責管理

The department was badly organized until she *took charge*.

☐ **take delight in** 喜歡 (= *delight in*)

Bill is fond of criticizing. He *takes delight in* pointing out others' weaknesses.

☐ **take effect** 生效

His new appointment *takes effect* from the beginning of next month.

☐ **take…for** 把…誤認為 (= *mistake…for*)

I *took* her *for* her sister. They look so much alike.

☐ **take great pains** 非常努力

The farmer *took great pains* to persuade those tourists to buy his farm products.

☐ **take hold of** 抓住；得到（= *grasp*）

She was lucky to *take hold of* a block of shares before the price went up.

☐ **take…into account** 考慮到

I'd *take into account* his reputation with other farmers and business people in the community, and then make a decision about whether or not to approve a loan.

☐ **take it easy** 放輕鬆（= *relax*）

Don't let anything bother you. Just *take it easy*.

☐ **take leave of** 向…道別

He *took leave of* me and started on his trip.

☐ **take off** 起飛

Three airplanes *took off* at the same time.

☐ **take off** 脫掉

Helen *took off* her coat because the room was too warm.

☐ **take on** 雇用 (= *hire*)

We will have to *take on* someone to do John's work while he is away.

☐ **take** *one's* **time** 慢慢來

There is no need to rush; just *take your time*.

🏛 Check List

☐ take off _____

☐ take it easy _____

☐ take charge _____

☐ take leave of _____

☐ take on _____

☐ take after _____

☐ take delight in _____

☐ take…into account _____

☐ take effect _____

☐ take advantage of _____

☐ take…for _____

☐ take apart _____

☐ take great pains _____

☐ take hold of _____

☐ take *one's* time _____

同義成語

1. *take account of*
   = take…into account
   = take…into consideration
   = allow for
   = make allowance for
   = consider
   考慮到

2. *take after*
   = look like
   = bear a resemblance to
   = have a resemblance to
   = be similar to
   = resemble
   相像

3. *take advantage of*
   = make use of
   = avail *oneself* of
   利用

4. *take care of*
   = care for
   = look after
   = see after
   = attend to
   = watch over
   = keep an eye on
   照顧

5. *take effect*
   = come into effect
   = go into effect
   = come into force
   = be in force
   生效

···✦ STEP 39 ✦···

☐ **take** *one's* **word for it** 相信某人的話

This is exactly what happened. *Take my word for it.*

☐ **take over** 接管

It is a common theme in many science fiction stories that the world may one day be *taken over* by insects.

☐ **take part in** 參加 (= *participate in*)

I am not interested in the subject and I don't want to *take part in* their argument.

☐ **take pity on** 同情

Many people *took pity on* those orphans whose parents died during the "921 Earthquake" and adopted them.

☐ **take place** 舉行；發生

The summit meeting between the presidents of those two countries *took place* in Paris last week.

☐ **take pride in** 以～為榮

The father *takes* much *pride in* his smart son.

☐ **take** *sb.* **at** *sb.'s* **word** 相信某人的話

Take me at my word. I will never break my promise.

☐ **take** *sb.* **by surprise** 使某人驚訝

The amount of the donation *took us* completely *by surprise*.

☐ **take** *sb.* **in** 欺騙某人 (= *deceive sb.*)

Be careful. Don't be *taken in* by people who try to mislead you.

☐ **take sides**　表明立場

In my opinion, it's important not to *take sides* in this kind of political dispute.

☐ **take** *sth.* **for granted**
把某事視爲理所當然

I am sick of being *taken for granted*. I've done so much but no one here shows any appreciation.

☑ **take** *sth.* **in stride**　從容地應付某事

He did it on purpose. However, I *took it in stride* instead of being irritated by him.

☐ **take** *sth.* **up with** *sb.*
向某人請教某事

I can't answer your questions; go see the supervisor and *take them up with him*.

☐ **take** *sth.* **with a grain of salt**
對某事持保留的態度

He is always bragging about what he has done, so we must *take* his words *with a grain of salt*.

☐ **take the words out of** *one's* **mouth** 搶先說出某人要講的話

I was going to say that we should go to the movies, but you *took the words out of my mouth*.

☐ **take to** *one's* **heels** 逃走

When he heard the police coming, the thief *took to his heels*.

☐ **take turns** 輪流

On the way to our destination, we *took turns* driving the car.

🏛 Check List

☐ take *sth.* in stride _____

☐ take *one's* word for it _____

☐ take place _____

☐ take *sb.* by surprise _____

☐ take over _____

☐ take turns _____

☐ take to *one's* heels _____

☐ take pity on _____

☐ take pride in _____

☐ take *sth.* for granted _____

☐ take *sb.* in _____

☐ take part in _____

☐ take *sb.* at *sb.'s* word _____

☐ take sides _____

☐ take *one's* time _____

📑 同義成語

1. *take off* 脫掉
   = pull off
   = peel off

2. *take part in*
   = take a hand in
   = take a share in
   = have a share in
   = participate in
   = sit in on
   參加

3. *take sth. up with sb.*
   = talk sth. over with sb.
   = consult sb. about sth.
   向某人請教某事

4. *take sb. in*
   = lead sb. on
   = string sb. along
   = do a snow job on sb.
   = put sth. over on sb.
   = deceive sb.
   欺騙某人

5. *take sth. with a grain of salt*
   = take sth. with a pinch of salt
   對某事持保留的態度

6. *take to one's heels*
   = take wing
   = run away
   = run off
   逃走

⋯⋆ STEP 40 ⋆⋯

☐ **take up** 佔據

Hospital doctors don't go out very often as their work *takes up* all their time.

☐ **talk over** 討論（ = *discuss* ）

I *talked over* the plan with my colleagues but could not come to a decision.

☐ **talk** *sb.* **into doing** *sth.*
說服某人做某事

I *talked* her *into* marrying him.

☐ **tear down** 拆除（ = *demolish* ）

The old museum is to be torn down and replaced by a brand-new office building.

☐ **tell…apart** 分辨 (= *distinguish*)

The two brothers are identical twins. Even their mother finds it hard to *tell* them *apart*.

☐ **think better of it** 改變主意

He was tempted to argue, but *thought better of it*.

☐ **think of A as B** 認爲 A 是 B

We *think of* Mike *as* a good student because he studies hard and does well on all the tests.

☐ **think over** 仔細考慮 (= *ponder*)

Think over the plan carefully, and let me know your decision.

☐ **throw cold water on** 潑冷水；不贊成

Henry's father *threw cold water on* his plans to go to college by saying that he could not afford it.

☐ **throw up** 嘔吐 (= *vomit*)

Dozens of people who attended the wedding banquet *threw up* after the party.

☐ **tidy up** 整理；使整潔

After the guests left, she spent half an hour *tidying up* the living room.

☐ **tighten** *one's* **belt** 節儉度日

Whenever I run out of money at the end of the month, I have to *tighten my belt* until the next payday.

☐ **tire out** 使筋疲力盡

He was *tired out* after his long trip to California.

☐ **top off** 完成；結束

They *topped off* the evening with a display of fireworks.

☐ **touch down** 降落 (= *land*)

His jumbo jet is due to *touch down* on the runway at noon.

☐ **touch on** 簡單帶過

Because of the time limit, just *touch on* this matter. Don't discuss it in detail.

☐ **track down** 追蹤到；追查到

It's hard for the abandoned child to *track down* her mother after so long a time.

☐ **trade in** 以舊品抵價購買

She *traded in* her Besta CD-85 for a new model.

Check List

- [ ] tighten *one's* belt　＿＿＿＿＿＿＿
- [ ] tell…apart　＿＿＿＿＿＿＿
- [ ] throw cold water on　＿＿＿＿＿＿＿
- [ ] take up　＿＿＿＿＿＿＿
- [ ] throw up　＿＿＿＿＿＿＿

- [ ] track down　＿＿＿＿＿＿＿
- [ ] top off　＿＿＿＿＿＿＿
- [ ] talk over　＿＿＿＿＿＿＿
- [ ] think better of it　＿＿＿＿＿＿＿
- [ ] touch on　＿＿＿＿＿＿＿

- [ ] trade in　＿＿＿＿＿＿＿
- [ ] tear down　＿＿＿＿＿＿＿
- [ ] think over　＿＿＿＿＿＿＿
- [ ] talk *sb*. into doing *sth*.　＿＿＿＿＿＿＿
- [ ] think of A as B　＿＿＿＿＿＿＿

同義成語

1. **talk** *sb.* **into doing** *sth.*
   = argue *sb.* into doing *sth.*
   = reason *sb.* into doing *sth.*

   = persuade *sb.* to do *sth.*
   = prevail on *sb.* to do *sth.*

   說服某人做某事

2. **tear down**
   = pull down

   = demolish
   = destroy

   拆除

3. **think of** A **as** B
   = look upon A as B
   = regard A as B

   = consider A (to be) B
   = think A (to be) B

   認為 A 是 B

···* STEP 41 *···

☑ **try out** 徹底試驗

The idea seems good, but it needs to be *tried out*.

☑ **turn a deaf ear to** 完全不聽

Mrs. Lin *turned a deaf ear to* her husband's complaints because, to her, facing the music is more constructive than complaining all day.

☑ **turn aside** 使轉變方向 (= *deflect*)

Light rays are *turned aside* by the intense gravitational field surrounding a black hole.

☑ **turn down** 拒絕 (= *reject*)

Peter made a proposal to Helen, but she *turned* him *down*.

☐ **turn down** 關小聲

Would you be good enough to *turn down* the radio a bit? It's too loud.

☐ **turn in** 繳交

You must *turn in* your gun when you leave the army.

☐ **turn in** 就寢

It's very late and I'm very tired. If you don't mind, I think I'll *turn in* now.

☐ **turn on** 使人產生興趣 (= *interest*)

Mozart's music always *turns* me *on*.

☐ **turn** *one's* **back on** 拒絕

I can't believe that Al *turned his back on* his mother when she needed his help.

☐ **turn out** 出現 (= *show up*)

How many people *turned out* for the
baseball game yesterday?

☐ **turn out** 結果 (成為)

Sometimes things don't *turn out* the way
we think they are going to.

☐ **turn over** 移交 (= *transfer*)

The father has decided to *turn over* his
business to his only son.

☐ **turn over** 翻轉

Turn over two of the cards at a time, and
see if they match.

☐ **turn over a new leaf** 重新做人；
改過自新

Every New Year we make resolutions to
turn over a new leaf.

☐ **turn to** *sb*. 向某人求助

The child felt there was no one he could *turn to* with his problems.

☐ **turn up** 出現 (= *show up*)

I waited an hour for him, but he didn't *turn up*.

☐ **upset the applecart**
破壞計劃；打亂步驟

Those senators may have a personal interest in passing the bill, so they are unwilling to *upset the applecart* even under the pressure of their supporters.

☐ **use up** 用完

I'm afraid that all of the cheap sources of energy will be *used up* in the future.

🏛 Check List

- ☐ turn aside _____
- ☐ turn over a new leaf _____
- ☐ try out _____
- ☐ turn down _____
- ☐ turn *one's* back on _____

- ☐ turn to *sb.* _____
- ☐ turn a deaf ear to _____
- ☐ turn in _____
- ☐ turn up _____
- ☐ upset the applecart _____

- ☐ turn out _____
- ☐ turn on _____
- ☐ turn over _____
- ☐ use up _____

同義成語

1. *turn down*
   = pass up
   = reject
   = refuse
   = decline
   拒絕

2. *turn in*
   = hand in
   = submit
   繳交

3. *turn in*
   = go to bed
   = hit the hay
   = hit the sack
   就寢

4. *turn up*
   = show up
   = turn out
   = come into sight
   = present *oneself*
   = make an appearance
   = enter an appearance
   = appear
   出現

⋅⋅⋅ STEP 42 ⋅⋅⋅

☐ **used to V.** 以前

It *used to* be thought that the earth was flat.

☐ **wait on** 服務；伺候（ = *serve* ）

The waitress politely asked, "Have you been *waited on*, sir?"

☐ **wait up for** 熬夜等候

They are *waiting up for* their parents, who are arriving tonight.

☐ **wake up** 醒來（ = *awake* ）

Not knowing why, I *woke up* in the early hours and could not fall asleep again.

☐ **ward off** 避免（= *avoid*）

Stricter measures have been taken to *ward off* potential dangers concerning cigarette smoking.

☐ **wear away** 磨損

Abrasives are sharp, hard materials used to *wear away* the surface of softer, less resistant materials.

☐ **wear off** （藥效）逐漸消失

The medicine is *wearing off*; my head is starting to hurt again.

☐ **wear out** 穿壞；磨損；使筋疲力盡

Some of the tapes in the language lab have been *worn out* and should be replaced.

□ **whoop it up**　狂歡 (= *paint the town red*)

Hey, let's get rowdy. Let's *whoop it up*.

□ **wind up with**　以～作為結束

If you keep spending money like this,
you'll *wind up with* nothing.

□ **wipe out**　徹底毀滅

The rescue team hurried to the town
wiped out by the earthquake to search
for survivors.

□ **work on**　致力於 (= *make efforts at*)

Scientists are still *working on* new
methods of reaching far outer space,
beyond the moon and Mars.

□ **work overtime**　加班

Since Fred arrived late, now he is *working
overtime* to finish his assignments.

☐ **work up** 激起（情緒）

A really powerful speaker can *work up* the feelings of the audience to a fever of excitement.

☐ **worry about** 擔心

"I'm sorry I've spilt some milk on the tablecloth."

"Oh, don't *worry about* that."

☐ **wrap up** 完成；結束（= *complete* ）

Before going abroad, the businessman had to *wrap up* his affairs.

☐ **yield to** 向～屈服（= *give in to* ）

He *yielded to* her ardent wishes.

📖 Check List

- [ ] wind up with _____
- [ ] yield to _____
- [ ] wipe out _____
- [ ] wrap up _____
- [ ] work on _____

- [ ] worry about _____
- [ ] work up _____
- [ ] work overtime _____
- [ ] used to V. _____
- [ ] wait up for _____

- [ ] wear off _____
- [ ] wake up _____
- [ ] wear out _____
- [ ] ward off _____
- [ ] wait on _____

📑 同義成語

1. **wait on**
   = attend
   = serve
   服務；伺候

2. **wind up with**
   = end up with
   = finish up with
   以～作為結束

3. **wipe out**
   = root out
   = destroy
   徹底毀滅

4. **yield to**
   = give up to
   = give in to
   = give way to
   = give *oneself* up to
   = surrender to
   向～屈服

PART 3 形容詞用法的成語

⋯⋆ STEP 43 ⋆⋯

☐ **a good many** 很多（ = *many* ）

There have been *a good many* protests against the new project.

☐ **as cool as a cucumber** 非常冷靜

Jack keeps calm even in an emergency. He is *as cool as a cucumber*.

☐ **a series of** 一連串的

The older polio vaccine had to be given in *a series of* injections.

☐ **as fit as a fiddle** 非常健康

Though past 70, my grandfather is still *as fit as a fiddle*. He looks much younger than his age.

☐ **at ease** 舒適；自在的 (= *comfortable*)

He didn't feel *at ease* in the strange surroundings.

☐ **at large** 逍遙法外的

The escaped prisoner is still *at large*. The police are looking everywhere for him.

☐ **at** *one's* **disposal** 任由某人支配

When I became a high-ranking executive, the firm put a secretary *at my disposal*.

☐ **at stake** 瀕臨危險的 (= *at risk*)

We should help him immediately, because his life is *at stake*.

☐ **be above + V-ing** 不屑於~

They are very honest; they *are above taking* bribes.

☐ **be all ears**　洗耳恭聽；專心聽

Go ahead with your story; we *are all ears*.

☐ **be all the vogue**　大為流行；風靡一時

Cellular phones have become *all the vogue* for people of every generation.

☐ **be all thumbs**　笨手笨腳

(= *be clumsy*)

When I do the dishes, I *am all thumbs*.

☐ **be at a loss**　茫然不知所措；困惑

I *was at a* complete *loss* as to how I could solve the problem.

☐ **be at odds**　不合；爭吵

Matt had a dispute with the general manager again. They have *been at odds* for a long time.

☐ **be at** *one's* **wit's end** 無計可施

No one will help him, and now he *is at his wit's end*.

☐ **be at the end of** *one's* **rope**
山窮水盡；無計可施

With all her savings gone and bills piling up, she *was at the end of her rope*.

☐ **be beside** *oneself* 欣喜若狂

They *were beside themselves* with joy after they had beaten their rivals in basketball.

☐ **be characteristic of** 是…的特色

Overcrowding *is characteristic of* urban slums.

☐ **be frozen to death** 被凍死

It was so cold that many animals *were frozen to death*.

Check List

- [ ] at stake
- [ ] be above + V-ing
- [ ] at large
- [ ] be characteristic of
- [ ] be all thumbs

- [ ] be at *one's* wit's end
- [ ] at ease
- [ ] be at a loss
- [ ] be all the vogue
- [ ] at *one's* disposal

- [ ] as fit as a fiddle
- [ ] be frozen to death
- [ ] be all ears
- [ ] be at odds
- [ ] a series of

同義成語

1. *as cool as a cucumber*
   非常冷靜
   as fit as a fiddle
   非常健康
   as busy as a bee
   非常忙碌
   as sly as a fox
   非常狡猾

2. *at one's disposal*
   = at the disposal of *one*
   任由某人處置

3. *be all ears* 專心聽
   be all eyes 專心看
   be all smiles
   滿臉笑容
   be all thumbs
   笨手笨腳

4. *be at a loss*
   = be at sea
   = be bewildered
   = be puzzled
   = be confused
   = be perplexed
   = be mixed up
   茫然不知所措；困惑

5. *be at one's wit's end*
   = be at the end of *one's* rope
   = be at the end of *one's* tether
   無計可施

⋯✦ STEP 44 ✦⋯

☐ **be in keeping with** 與⋯一致

The goals of our education system *are in keeping with* the development of our society.

☐ **be in the habit of + V-ing** 習慣於

Tom *is in the habit of* going to bed at eleven.

☐ **be in the same boat** 處境相同

She and I *are in the same boat*; we both failed the exam and were scolded by the teacher.

☐ **be near at hand** 逼近；就快到了

He studied very hard because the final exam *was near at hand*.

☐ **be on the inside track** 處於有利地位

You *are on the inside track*. The situation is to your advantage. Make good use of it, and you will succeed.

☐ **be out of** *one's* **mind** 發瘋

Anyone who is willing to descend into the monster's cave must *be out of his mind*.

☐ **be reduced to a skeleton** 皮包骨

The poor old man *was reduced to* just *a skeleton*.

☐ **be tied up** 忙得無法分身

I'm sorry I can't come to the party this evening. I'*m tied up* at the office.

☐ **behind the times** 落伍

Grandfather's ideas are really *behind the times*. They are out-of-date.

☐ **beside the point**　離題的

His criticism was totally *beside the point* but he thought he was hitting the nail on the head.

☐ **better off**　（經濟情況）更好（ = *richer* ）

After many years of hard work, they became *better off*.

☐ **beyond retrieval**　無法挽回

The situation is now *beyond retrieval*. We cannot but give it up.

☐ **down to earth**　實際的（ = *practical* ）

He's young; but compared with his friends, he's more *down to earth*.

☐ **few and far between**
間隔很遠的；稀少的

In this sparsely-populated area, houses are *few and far between*.

☐ **half the size of** 大小是～的一半

The bird is *half the size of* an eagle.

☐ **in a bad mood** 心情不好

Father was *in a bad mood* since he couldn't play golf because of bad weather.

☐ **in a fog** 困惑的；如墜入五里霧中

When people are confused, they can say they are *in a fog*.

☐ **in a litter** 亂七八糟；雜亂的

She was ashamed to ask me in, for her room was *in a litter*.

☐ **in deep water** 陷入困境

Having lost her passport, she is now *in deep water*.

Check List

☐ in a litter _____

☐ down to earth _____

☐ be in keeping with _____

☐ be on the inside track _____

☐ in a fog _____

☐ beyond retrieval _____

☐ be out of *one's* mind _____

☐ be in the same boat _____

☐ in a bad mood _____

☐ better off _____

☐ be tied up _____

☐ be near at hand _____

☐ half the size of _____

☐ beside the point _____

☐ in deep water _____

同義成語

1.
    be in keeping with
    = be in line with
    = be at one with

    = be in accord with
    = be in harmony
      with

    = fall into line with
    = fit in with

    = see eye to eye
      with
    = agree with

    與…一致

2.
    be in the habit of
    = have the habit of

    = be accustomed to
    = be used to

    習慣於

3.
    be out of one's
    mind
    = be out of *one's*
      head

    = be off *one's* head
    = have a bee in
      one's bonnet
    = lose *one's* mind

    = be nuts
    = be crazy

    發瘋

4.
    in deep water
    = in hot water

    = in a jam
    = in a fix
    = in trouble

    陷入困境

⋅ ⋆ STEP 45 ⋆ ⋅

☑ **in effect** 有效的；在實施中

Though a cease-fire was *in effect*, there were still reports of violence in some areas.

☑ **in full bloom** 盛開的

With the coming of spring, all things revive and flowers are *in full bloom*.

☑ **in question** 討論中的

The college *in question* is one of the best in our country. You may apply to it for admission.

☑ **in ruins** 成為廢墟

The city of Berlin was *in ruins* at the end of the war.

☐ **in shape** 身體健康 (= *in condition*)

I began jogging every morning before work in order to stay *in shape*.

☐ **in the bag** 十拿九穩的；一定能成功

With her talent and hard work, Susie's success is *in the bag*.

☐ **in the dark** 不知道的

Mickey is *in the dark* about our plans to throw a surprise birthday party for him.

☐ **in the pink** 非常健康

The children all looked *in the pink* because of well-balanced nutrition and exercise.

☐ **in trouble** 有麻煩

Kevin is *in trouble* because he broke the living room window this afternoon.

☐ **in vogue**　流行的

That style is no longer *in vogue*.

☐ **off the point**　離題

You are talking nonsense, Jack. What you have said is quite *off the point*.

☐ **on pins and needles**　坐立難安

I saw a horror movie last night called "Scream 3." This movie will keep you *on pins and needles* from beginning to end.

☐ **on the blink**　故障的

The new photocopier is *on the blink*. It must have been damaged during shipping.

☐ **on the go**　忙個不停的

Everyone in the industrialized society seems to be busy and constantly *on the go*.

☐ **on the house** 免費的

I like to go to my friend's bar because the drinks are always *on the house*.

☐ **on the rocks** 觸礁；瀕臨破裂

Willy's marriage is *on the rocks*. His wife has decided to file for a divorce next week.

☐ **out of breath** 喘不過氣

The old lady was *out of breath* from climbing up the stairs.

☐ **out of date** 過時的 (= *outdated*)

He claims to be an expert on the subject but his knowledge is *out of date* and inaccurate.

☐ **out of hand** 無法控制

If things get *out of hand*, you should call me immediately.

🏛 Check List

☐ out of breath   _____

☐ off the point   _____

☐ in the dark   _____

☐ in question   _____

☐ on the rocks   _____

☐ in vogue   _____

☐ in the bag   _____

☐ out of hand   _____

☐ on the house   _____

☐ in shape   _____

☐ in trouble   _____

☐ on the go   _____

☐ on the blink   _____

☐ in the pink   _____

☐ out of date   _____

📖 同義成語

1. *in the pink*
   = in good shape
   = in good
     condition
   非常健康

2. *in vogue*
   = in fashion
   = in style
   流行的

3. *out of date*
   = out of fashion
   = out of style
   = behind the times
   落伍

4. *out of hand*
   = out of control
   失去控制

5. *off the point*
   = beside the point
   = away from the
     point
   = not to the point
   = beside the
     question
   = beside the mark
   = neither here nor
     there
   = off the subject
   = irrelevant
   離題的

6. *on the blink*
   = out of order
   = broken
   故障的

⟨ ★ STEP 46 ★ ⟩

☐ **out of order** 故障的

Why didn't you tell me the vending machine was *out of order*?

☐ **out of place** 不適當 (= *unsuitable*)

His behavior at the party seemed rather *out of place*. Many of us were quite surprised.

☐ **out of print** 絕版

If you order a book from a bookstore, but it is no longer available from the publisher, then this book is *out of print* now.

☐ **out of the question** 不可能

The summer campers thought that snow as late as June was *out of the question*.

☐ **out of tune** 音調不準

The band sounded terrible, because the instruments were *out of tune*.

☐ **out of work** 失業 (= *jobless*)

Jack is at present *out of work*, so he has difficulty paying his car installments.

☐ **quite a few** 很多 (= *many*)

Quite a few students were absent yesterday due to the flood.

☐ **ten to one** 十之八九；八成

It is *ten to one* that he'll be late, as is usual with him.

☐ **the last** 最不可能的

He is very ambitious. He would be *the last* person to resign from the post of his own accord.

□ **to the point** 切題；切中要點

Your speech this afternoon was much too
long and a little too vague. Next time you
should make it shorter and more *to the
point*.

□ **true to life** 寫實的；與實際生活相同的

The story he wrote is *true to life*.
Everybody is wondering whom he
was referring to.

□ **under way** 進行中

Formal negotiations between the two
major companies are *under way*.

□ **up and about** 康復

Last week May was in the hospital, but
I've heard that she's *up and about* now
and will soon be back at work.

☑ **up for grabs** 供人競爭；待價而沽

They've decided to change their advertising company, so a big contract is *up for grabs*.

☑ **up in the air** 未決定；尚不確定

Because the election isn't certain yet, who will become the country's next president is still *up in the air*.

☑ **up to date** 最新的；流行的

The book has been revised and brought *up to date*.

☑ **worlds apart** 完全不同的

The main reason why the couple broke up was that their thoughts were *worlds apart*.

🏛 Check List

- ☐ under way _____
- ☐ ten to one _____
- ☐ out of print _____
- ☐ up and about _____
- ☐ true to life _____

- ☐ quite a few _____
- ☐ out of place _____
- ☐ up for grabs _____
- ☐ out of work _____
- ☐ to the point _____

- ☐ out of tune _____
- ☐ out of order _____
- ☐ up to date _____
- ☐ the last _____
- ☐ out of the question _____

同義成語

1. *out of the question*
   = impossible
   不可能

   cf. *out of question*
   = beyond question
   = past question
   = without question
   沒問題

2. *quite a few*
   = not a few
   = a number of
   = a lot of
   = a good many
   = a great many
   = many
   很多

3. *to the point*
   = to the subject
   = relevant
   切題

4. *out of work*
   = jobless
   = unemployed
   失業

5. *up and about*
   = up and around
   康復

6. *worlds apart*
   = completely
      different
   完全不同的

PART 4 ▶ 其他用法的成語

⟨• **STEP 47** •⟩

☐ **a back-seat driver** 坐在後座指揮開
車的人；愛管閒事的人
She was *a back-seat driver*; she repeatedly
gave advice without being asked for it.

☐ **a bird of passage** 候鳥；漂泊不定的人
He is *a bird of passage*, always here today
and gone tomorrow.

☐ **a drop in the bucket** 滄海一粟；
於事無補
I tried my best to help, but it was just *a
drop in the bucket*.

☐ **a fish out of water** 如魚出水；不得
其所的人
She was the only girl at the party not in a
formal dress and she felt like *a fish out of
water*.

☐ **a fly in the ointment**　美中不足的事

We had a lot of fun at the beach; the only *fly in the ointment* was George's cutting his foot on a piece of glass.

☐ **a green thumb**　園藝的才能

Martha's garden is beautiful; she has *a green thumb*.

☐ **a man of his word**　守信用的人

The pianist is *a man of his word*. He promised the audience that he would play his most famous song, and he did play it for the encore.

☐ **a man of letters**　文學家；學者

Mr. White has a wide knowledge of literature; he is *a man of letters*.

☐ **a narrow escape**　驚險的逃脫

More than once he had *a narrow escape* from being eaten by sharks.

☐ **a pain in the neck**　討厭鬼

I got very angry when Fred played a trick on me. He is really *a pain in the neck*.

☐ **a straight face**　面無表情

Despite Lucy's jokes, Andy sat there with *a straight face*.

☐ **a wet blanket**　煞風景的人或物

The teenagers don't invite Jimmy to their parties because he is *a wet blanket*.

☐ **black sheep**　害群之馬；敗家子

There is a *black sheep* in every flock.

☐ **brain trust**　智囊團

A *brain trust* is a group of experts who serve as consultants on strategy.

☐ **census data**　人口普查

According to the recent *census data*, there are over 23 million people in Taiwan.

☑ **dark horse** 黑馬

She is a bit of a *dark horse*; she might win the race after all.

☑ **every walk of life** 各行各業

Bob is a reporter and often has contact with people from *every walk of life*.

☑ **food for thought** 值得思考的問題

The speaker's lecture was quite stimulating. It has given us some *food for thought*.

☑ **give-and-take** 交換意見

In radio and television call-in programs, there is a lot of *give-and-take* between the host and audience.

☑ **leg work** 跑腿的工作

Joe, my research assistant, does a lot of *leg work* for me.

☑ **life span** 壽命

Some insects have a *life span* of no more than a few hours.

☑ **long shot** 希望不大

I left my wallet in the taxi this morning. I know it's a *long shot* in such a greedy society, but I still should ask at the police station if anyone has handed it in.

☑ **odds and ends** 零星雜物

I've taken most of the big things to the new house, but there are a few *odds and ends* left to collect.

☑ *one's* **cup of tea** 喜愛的事物或活動

It is unlikely that she will win the championship in figure skating, because it is not *her cup of tea*.

□ **Prince Charming** 白馬王子

She is really picky about choosing her boyfriend. She's still waiting for her *Prince Charming*.

□ **rain check** 改期；補請

I can't go with you to the party tomorrow, but I will take a *rain check*. Maybe next time.

□ **second thoughts** 重新考慮；三思

Do you really want to give it up? No *second thoughts*?

□ **the ins and outs** 細節；詳情

Ask him if you have any questions. He is in charge of this case and he knows all *the ins and outs*.

□ **wear and tear** 磨損；耗損

David won't buy that old machine because it has too much *wear and tear*.

🏛 Check List

- ☐ a bird of passage　＿＿＿＿＿＿
- ☐ a green thumb　＿＿＿＿＿＿
- ☐ a straight face　＿＿＿＿＿＿
- ☐ every walk of life　＿＿＿＿＿＿
- ☐ a drop in the bucket　＿＿＿＿＿＿

- ☐ a man of his word　＿＿＿＿＿＿
- ☐ a wet blanket　＿＿＿＿＿＿
- ☐ food for thought　＿＿＿＿＿＿
- ☐ a fish out of water　＿＿＿＿＿＿
- ☐ a narrow escape　＿＿＿＿＿＿

- ☐ black sheep　＿＿＿＿＿＿
- ☐ a man of letters　＿＿＿＿＿＿
- ☐ a fly in the ointment　＿＿＿＿＿＿
- ☐ a pain in the neck　＿＿＿＿＿＿
- ☐ brain trust　＿＿＿＿＿＿

📖 同義成語

1. *a drop in the bucket*
   = a drop in the ocean
   滄海一粟；於事無補

2. *a green thumb*
   = green fingers
   園藝的才能

3. *a narrow escape*
   = a close call
   = a close shave
   驚險的逃脫

4. *a pain in the neck*
   = a pain in the ass
   討厭鬼

5. *black sheep*
   害群之馬
   dark horse 黑馬
   loan shark
   放高利貸的人
   jailbird 囚犯
   early bird
   早起的人

6. *brain trust*
   = think tank
   智囊團

7. *every walk of life*
   = all walks of life
   各行各業

8. *Prince Charming*
   = Mr. Right
   白馬王子

✦ STEP 48 ✦

☐ **according to** 根據

According to the weather forecast tonight, the temperature will drop tomorrow.

☐ **across from** 在～對面（= *opposite*）

The couple sitting *across from* me are having an argument.

☐ **apart from** 除了～之外還有

Apart from other considerations, time is a factor.

☐ **as a result of** 因為；由於

As a result of all the newspaper and television attention, the problem of child abuse has become well-known.

☑ **as to** 關於 (= *about*)

There was no doubt *as to* who the man was.

☑ **at the cost of** 以～的代價；犧牲

Jacky was so delighted to have the job that he worked *at the cost of* his health.

☑ **at the mercy of** 受～的支配

Farmers are always *at the mercy of* the weather.

☑ **by means of** 藉由；利用 (= *by*)

He solved the problem *by means of* simple equations.

☑ **by way of** 經由 (= *by the route of*)

I am thinking of going to Poland *by way of* Siberia.

☐ **except for** 除了～之外

Except for the Joneses, I don't know anybody in this village.

☐ **for all** 儘管 (= *in spite of*)

For all their differences, the couple was developing an obvious and genuine affection for each other.

☐ **for the sake of** 看在～的份上；為了

For the sake of our friendship, do not argue with me about this.

☐ **in case of** 萬一有～情況

In case of fire, please use the stairway instead of the elevator.

☐ **in competition for** 爭奪

A total of thirty teams from 10 countries joined in the tournament *in competition for* the championship.

☐ **in favor of** 贊成 (= *for*)

Most of the union members were *in favor of* the proposal to go on strike.

☐ **in honor of** 紀念

When Edison died, it was proposed that the American people turn off all power for several minutes *in honor of* this great man.

☐ **in place of** 代替

I'd like you to write a term paper *in place of* a final exam.

☐ **in proportion to** 與~成比例

It is a well-known fact that one's success is *in proportion to* one's work.

☐ **in relation to** 關於 (= *with regard to*)

In relation to the effort we had made, the reward we got was too little.

Check List

- [ ] according to　＿＿＿＿＿＿
- [ ] as to　＿＿＿＿＿＿
- [ ] for all　＿＿＿＿＿＿
- [ ] in favor of　＿＿＿＿＿＿
- [ ] across from　＿＿＿＿＿＿

- [ ] at the mercy of　＿＿＿＿＿＿
- [ ] for the sake of　＿＿＿＿＿＿
- [ ] in honor of　＿＿＿＿＿＿
- [ ] apart from　＿＿＿＿＿＿
- [ ] by means of　＿＿＿＿＿＿

- [ ] in case of　＿＿＿＿＿＿
- [ ] in place of　＿＿＿＿＿＿
- [ ] as a result of　＿＿＿＿＿＿
- [ ] by way of　＿＿＿＿＿＿
- [ ] in competition for　＿＿＿＿＿＿

同義成語

1. *apart from*
   = aside from
   = in addition to
   = besides
   除了～之外還有

2. *as to* 關於
   = as for
   = with regard to
   = with relation to
   = with reference to
   = in regard to
   = in relation to
   = in reference to
   = in respect to
   = with respect to
   = in connection with
   = respecting
   = regarding
   = concerning
   = about

3. *at the cost of*
   = at the expense of
   = at the loss of
   以～的代價；犧牲

4. *at the mercy of*
   = at *one's* mercy
   = in the power of
   = under the control of
   受～的支配

5. *for all* 儘管
   = with all
   = in spite of
   = despite

6. *in honor of*
   = in memory of
   = in remembrance of 紀念

⋅ STEP 49 ⋅

☐ **in spite of** 儘管 (= *despite*)

In spite of the enemy's stubborn resistance, our army occupied the town as originally planned.

☐ **instead of** 不⋯而～；而不是

Instead of treating the homeless man as a shame of the society, Mrs. Wang provided him with food and water.

☐ **in terms of** 由～觀點看來

Einstein was one of the greatest scientists of the 20th century *in terms of* his influence on the study of physics.

☐ **in view of** 由於；有鑒於

In view of all the extra work at the office, I've decided to postpone my holiday.

☐ **next to** 幾乎 (= *almost*)

It's *next to* impossible for me to finish the homework in three days.

☐ **on account of** 因為；由於

The senator declined to give a speech *on account of* a sore throat.

☐ **on behalf of** 代表

Linda gave a thank-you speech to the teachers and parents *on behalf of* all the graduating students.

☐ **on the basis of** 以～為基礎

They have worked out a theory *on the basis of* recent research findings.

☐ **on the grounds of** 因為；由於

She did not participate in the activity *on the grounds of* her illness.

☐ **on the point of** 正要

She was *on the point of* taking a bath
when the telephone rang.

☐ **on the verge of** 瀕臨；即將

The man is *on the verge of* a serious
nervous breakdown because he is unable
to deal with the pressure of daily life.

☐ **other than** 除了～之外

In no country *other than* Britain, it has
been said, can one experience four
seasons in the course of a single day.

☐ **owing to** 由於 (= *due to*)

Owing to a scarcity of rain, this year's
rice crop will be poor.

☑ **regardless of** 不管～如何；無論

All living organisms, *regardless of* their unique identity, have certain biological, chemical, and physical characteristics in common.

☑ **thanks to** 由於 (= *due to*)

Our world is safer and more orderly *thanks to* the United Nations.

☑ **to say nothing of** 更不用說

He doesn't even drink beer, *to say nothing of* brandy.

☑ **with regard to** 至於；關於

With regard to your summer house, would you rent it to us next year?

🏛 Check List

☐ in spite of　　　　＿＿＿＿＿＿＿

☐ in view of　　　　＿＿＿＿＿＿＿

☐ on the basis of　　＿＿＿＿＿＿＿

☐ other than　　　　＿＿＿＿＿＿＿

☐ owing to　　　　　＿＿＿＿＿＿＿

☐ on the grounds of　＿＿＿＿＿＿＿

☐ next to　　　　　　＿＿＿＿＿＿＿

☐ instead of　　　　＿＿＿＿＿＿＿

☐ in terms of　　　　＿＿＿＿＿＿＿

☐ on account of　　　＿＿＿＿＿＿＿

☐ on the point of　　＿＿＿＿＿＿＿

☐ regardless of　　　＿＿＿＿＿＿＿

☐ thanks to　　　　　＿＿＿＿＿＿＿

☐ on the verge of　　＿＿＿＿＿＿＿

☐ on behalf of　　　　＿＿＿＿＿＿＿

同義成語

1. **in terms of**
    = with regard to
    = from the point
    of view of
    由～觀點看來

2. **on account of**
    = as a result of
    = on the grounds
    of
    = because of
    = due to
    = owing to
    = thanks to
    因爲；由於

3. **on the verge of**
    = on the brink of
    = on the border of
    = on the edge of
    瀕臨；即將

4. **other than**
    = else than
    = otherwise than
    = with the
    exception of
    = save
    = saving
    = except
    除了～之外

⋯⋆ STEP 50 ⋆⋯

☐ **as if** 就好像 (= *as though*)

I couldn't move my legs. It was *as if* they were stuck to the floor.

☐ **if only** 只要；如果～不知該有多好

I'm sure he is up to the job *if only* he would put his mind to it.

☐ **in case** 以防萬一

Take an umbrella with you *in case* it should rain.

☐ **it stands to reason that**
～是理所當然的

If you stay up late every night, *it stands to reason that* you will get sick.

☐ **let alone** 更不用說

For a country to survive, *let alone* to prosper, a good economic policy should be employed.

☐ **might as well…as～** 與其～不如…

We *might as well* pack up and go home *as* stay here.

☐ **much less** 更不用說

Most New Yorkers don't even own a gun, *much less* carry one around with them.

☐ **no more…than～** 和～一樣不…

He is *no more* able to read Spanish *than* I am.

☐ **now that** 既然 (= *since*)

Now that you mention money, it strikes me that you still owe me 2,000 dollars.

☑ **provided that** 如果

I will go to the meeting with you *provided that* I am free.

☑ **seeing that** 因為；由於

Seeing that it is eight o'clock, we'll wait no longer.

☑ **see that** 留意；注意 (= *see to it that*)

See that the door is locked.

☑ **the moment** 一～就…

The moment he heard the news, he rushed to the company.

☑ **what if** 如果～該怎麼辦

What if they should be thieves and steal goods from our store?

☐ **as far as I am concerned** 就我而言

She said she didn't like it, but *as far as I was concerned*, it was very good.

☐ **It figures**. 可以理解。

"John isn't here today."

"*It figures*. He looked very unwell yesterday."

☐ **…seldom, if ever,~**

即使曾經，也很少~

He is so hardworking that he *seldom, if ever*, goes to bed before midnight.

☐ **snap to it** 趕快

It's a rush job. *Snap to it*.

☐ **that makes two of us** 我也一樣

"I'm finding this party extremely dull."

"*That makes two of us*."

🏛 Check List

☐ ···seldom, if ever～ ＿＿＿＿＿＿＿＿＿

☐ might as well···as～ ＿＿＿＿＿＿＿＿＿

☐ let alone ＿＿＿＿＿＿＿＿＿

☐ if only ＿＿＿＿＿＿＿＿＿

☐ snap to it ＿＿＿＿＿＿＿＿＿

☐ provided that ＿＿＿＿＿＿＿＿＿

☐ see that ＿＿＿＿＿＿＿＿＿

☐ It figures. ＿＿＿＿＿＿＿＿＿

☐ with regard to ＿＿＿＿＿＿＿＿＿

☐ to say nothing of ＿＿＿＿＿＿＿＿＿

☐ now that ＿＿＿＿＿＿＿＿＿

☐ much less ＿＿＿＿＿＿＿＿＿

☐ seeing that ＿＿＿＿＿＿＿＿＿

☐ in case ＿＿＿＿＿＿＿＿＿

☐ what if ＿＿＿＿＿＿＿＿＿

同義成語

1. *if only*
   = on condition that
   = provided that
   = as long as
   = so long as
   只要

2. *to say nothing of*
   = not to speak of
   = not to mention
   = let alone
   = much more
   = still more
   = even more   肯定句
   = much less
   = still less
   = even less   否定句
   更不用說

3. *provided that*
   = providing that
   = supposing that
   = suppose that
   = if 如果

4. *the moment*
   = the instant
   = the minute
   = as soon as
   一…就~

5. *snap to it*
   = shake a leg
   = step on it
   = on the double
   = hurry up
   = hurry
   趕快

索 引

心得筆記欄

心得筆記欄

心得筆記欄

心得筆記欄

心得筆記欄

劉毅英文家教班同學獎學金排行榜

姓 名	學 校	總金額	姓 名	學 校	總金額	姓 名	學 校	總金額
潘羽薇	丹鳳高中	21100	廖奕翔	松山高中	8333	李泓霖	松山高中	5000
孔為亮	中崙高中	20000	蕭若浩	師大附中	8333	劉若白	大同高中	5000
吳文心	北一女中	17666	連偉宏	師大附中	8333	洪菀妤	師大附中	5000
賴柏盛	建國中學	17366	王舒亭	縣格致中學	8300	洪宇謙	成功高中	5000
劉記齊	建國中學	16866	楊政勳	中和高中	8100	黃柏誠	師大附中	5000
張庭碩	建國中學	16766	鄭鈺立	建國中學	8000	劉其瑄	中山女中	5000
陳瑾慧	北一女中	16700	吳宇晏	南港高中	8000	陳韋廷	成功高中	5000
羅培恩	建國中學	16666	楊沐焓	師大附中	7750	李維任	成功高中	5000
毛威凱	建國中學	16666	謝育姍	景美女中	7600	林晉陽	師大附中	4900
王辰方	北一女中	16666	高士權	建國中學	7600	林品君	北一女中	4900
李俊逸	建國中學	16666	吳鴻鑫	中正高中	7333	柯季欣	華江高中	4500
溫彥瑾	建國中學	16666	謝宜廷	樹林高中	7000	李智傑	松山高中	4800
葉乃元	建國中學	16666	翁子惇	縣格致中學	6900	許博勳	松山高中	4300
邱御碩	建國中學	16666	朱浩廷	陽明高中	6500	張鈞堯	新北高中	4166
劉梧坤	松山高中	14400	張 毓	成淵高中	6500	林子薰	中山女中	4000
張凱俐	中山女中	13333	吳宇珊	景美女中	6200	里思予	林口高中	4000
邱譽荷	北一女中	12000	王昱期	延平高中	6200	鄭宇彤	樹林高中	4000
陳瑾瑜	北一女中	11700	張祐誠	林口高中	6100	張心瑜	格致高中	3900
施哲凱	松山高中	10450	游需晴	靜修女中	6000	賴奕均	松山高中	3900
陳宇翔	成功高中	10333	林彥君	大同高中	6000	戴寧昕	師大附中	3500
林上軒	政大附中	10000	張騰升	松山高中	6000	江紫寧	大同高中	3500
陳玟妤	中山女中	9000	陳姿穎	縣格致中學	5900	游清心	師大附中	3500
林泇欣	格致高中	8800	沈 怡	復興高中	5800	陳 犖	海山高中	3500
黃敦頤	大同高中	8600	莊永瑋	中壢高中	5600	曾清翎	板橋高中	3400
蘇玉如	北一女中	8400	邱鈺璸	成功高中	5600	吳昕儒	中正高中	3400
廖奕翔	松山高中	8333	許斯閔	丹鳳高中	5500	高正岳	方濟高中	3250
廖克軒	成功高中	8333	郭子豪	師大附中	5400	林夏竹	新北高中	3100
呂承翰	師大附中	8333	黃馪睿	東吳大學	5400	曾昭惠	永平高中	3000
鮑其鈺	師大附中	8333	陸冠宏	成功高中	5200	萬彰允	二信高中	3000
簡珞帆	高 中 生	8333	李柏霆	明倫高中	5100	張 晨	麗山國中	3000
蕭羽涵	松山高中	8333	孫廷瑋	成功高中	5100	廖泓恩	松山工農	3000

劉毅英文教育機構

台北市許昌街17號6F（捷運M8出口對面‧學養補習班）　　TEL：（02）2389-5212
台中市三民路三段125號7F（光南文具批發樓上‧劉毅補習班）　TEL：（04）2221-8861

升大學成語 1000

主　　　編／劉　毅

發　行　所／學習出版有限公司　　☎ (02) 2704-5525

郵　撥　帳　號／05127272 學習出版社帳戶

登　記　證／局版台業 2179 號

印　刷　所／裕強彩色印刷有限公司

台 北 門 市／台北市許昌街 10 號 2 F　　☎ (02) 2331-4060

台灣總經銷／紅螞蟻圖書有限公司　　☎ (02) 2795-3656

本公司網址　www.learnbook.com.tw

電 子 郵 件　learnbook@learnbook.com.tw

售價：新台幣二百二十元正

2017 年 6 月 1 日新修訂

4713269380573